Animalistic Desires

Complete 10 Part Paranormal Series

TRINITY STYLLER

Forbidden Lessons/ Trinity Styller. -- 1st ed.
Xplicit Press, an imprint of TLM Media LLC

ISBN-13: 978-1-62327-580-8
ISBN-10: 1-62327-580-6
eISBN: 978-1-62327-630-0

Printed in the United States of America

CONTENTS

1 THE FIRST MISSION

Water splashing down her back, Bailey stood in the shower, pressed up against the wall with her hands and feet sprawled out. Behind her, Draven ran his hands all over her tiny frame. God, how she loved the feel of his calloused hands on her body. Draven slowly teased her pussy with his fingers while holding her against the shower wall. Bailey was so glad he was home tonight.

She had learned to enjoy every minute that she had with him, because she never knew when he would be home again. Draven was in the military and was the head of some sort of special operations team. That was all that she knew about what he did, and that was all he wanted her to know. But she was about to find out how unique he really was.

Draven led his men to their next target: Bastian Alverez. He knew it would be difficult to get passed the mansion's high-tech alarm system undetected. There was one thing on his side – they had the element of surprise. But it wasn't just the alarm system they had to worry about; if he and his men were going to come out of this alive, they would have to avoid the bodyguards as well.

Draven knew that they had the best chance to get into the mansion when the skies were at their darkest. It was just after sunset; they only had a short time to prepare for the infiltration.

Back at home Bailey was planning for Draven's return. She could not wait until he was in her hands. The missions that the military sent him on were unbearable. But she knew that it was his job. She took her time, setting things up so that when he did arrive home he could not resist making love to her.

Bailey wore his favorite babydoll, made of a light blue satin and black lace, with a lacy black thong. He had bought it for her from her favorite lingerie store. Every once and a while, he would take the time to pick something out for her to wear while they were role-playing. But she liked to wear a garter or thong or peek-a-boo slip while she was cooking dinner for him, so she could pounce on him as soon as he walked in the kitchen.

Just as Bailey was bending over to pull out the pot roast and vegetables, she heard Draven enter the heavy front doors of the mansion. He went upstairs instead of coming into the kitchen like he usually did. She thought that was a little strange, but figured maybe he was in a hurry to change. She waited for him in the kitchen until he came downstairs.

Draven was a tall muscular man, power and strength suffusing all that he did. His only sign of weakness was a small scar above his left eye. He was wearing only a black velour robe. God, how she wanted him. He always looked amazing right after he came home from a mission. She slowly approached him, gazing into his green eyes.

Bailey wrapped her arms around his neck and began to kiss his neck gently, running her hands all over his muscular, tanned chest. She could feel the need building in his body. When she touched him, his body tensed up; as she pushed her body against his, she could feel his hard erection pushing against her.

Draven looked down at Bailey's bright, green eyes; he knew that she loved him just by the way that she took care of him without being asked. They had been together only eight months, but it seemed like they'd known each other forever.

He scooped her up, placing her on the island and began to have his way with her. He loved coming home to find her offering herself to him. He loved how she looked in that babydoll.

Draven began working his way down her neck and to her voluptuous breasts, teasing them with his tongue and then nipping at them with his teeth. He knew Bailey loved the way he used his teeth all over her body.

"God, how I missed you, Draven." She slowly ran her hands through his long, dark hair. Arching her body as she enjoyed every little touch from him, he looked up to her. This was all that he would do to her, but it was enough to sustain her for now.

Bailey could feel that there was something different about him tonight, but she could not put her finger on exactly what it was. He seemed distant and distracted. Was he going to tell her that he could not be with her anymore?

Draven knew that if he wanted to be with her that night, he would have to tell her exactly what he was, and what she would become if she were to join him. He stopped running his hands over her body and led her upstairs to their bedroom. Bailey was surprised and concerned, but she didn't asked questions.

The pot roast would keep.

When they reached the bedroom, Draven opened the door, picked her up and held her against his chest as he crossed the threshold into the room. Placing her on the bed gently, he walked around the room, lighting several candles and then stripping down to nothing. He lay down next to her. He ran his hands up and down her side, reveling in the feel of her soft skin and the silky babydoll. She was amazing to him.

"Bailey, I want to make love to you. The way my kind does once they find their mate."

She was not sure what he meant. What did he mean 'the way that his kind did'? What exactly was 'his kind'?

She wanted Draven so badly, but she was also nervous and confused. But before she could even think, one word escaped past her lips. "Yes

Draven looked at her in awe. "Yes? But you do not know anything about my way. How can you just say you will do it if you do not know anything about my family traditions?" He looked at her, puzzled. Did he really mean that much to her, that she would do anything for him? Only time would tell if she was true to her word.

"Bailey, do you trust me?"

Looking at him with those innocent, green eyes, she ran her hands over his bare, muscular chest. Draven thought that she was the most beautiful creature he had ever seen. Every movement she made was fluid. He loved her. It was as simple as that.

Slowly, Bailey worked her way down to his hip bones, stopping and nipping at him, looking up at him mischievously. Draven loved it when she was up to no good. She began to take his cock in her mouth, swirling her tongue on its tip. God, she knew how to take his breath away. He had to have more.

He began moving his hips and wrapped his hands in her red hair, driving his cock deeper into her mouth. He was about to climax inside her mouth when he suddenly pulled his cock out. He slowly rose up to his hands and knees, crawling up between her legs, spreading them apart. God, she looked so sweet and innocent looking up at him. It was his turn to please her. Taking his time, he started kissing her ankles, working his way up to her calves and then to her inner thigh. He loved how she arched and wiggled underneath him. She began moaning as he kissed her body. It was as if her body was on fire; she was engulfed in flames and could not stop the heat from rising.

Draven placed one final kiss on her pelvic bone, looking up at her. "Bailey, please do not fear me or what is inside of me."

She knew that he would never harm her in any way, but still she watched him cautiously.

His body started to change; it became leaner and more muscular. A long tail grew out from the base of his spine.

She had wondered what she did not know about him. She was shocked at the transformation she was witnessing. At first, fear welled up within her. Not fear of him, but fear of not understanding what was happening. But then, it made her feel more protected that there was this muscular beast within Draven. Her fear quickly faded, replaced only with confusion.

Where a handsome man had lain beside her, there was not a beast, covered in sleek, thick fur. Its thick muscles tensed and flexed; its tail twitched anxiously. In front of her stood a magnificent black jaguar with green eyes.

But underneath it, she could see that it was him. She looked into those piercing eyes, and his form did not matter; she saw Draven in those majestic eyes. He slowly lowered his head and began licking her hand. As he nudged her hand, she began to rub his ears. Then Draven changed back into his normal self.

Seeing what Draven really was made Bailey love him more. She began kissing his lips, pulling his body on top of hers. "Draven, please make love to me, take me and make me part of you. I want to be with you, forever," she was begging.

He was elated with what he had heard. He felt as if his heart might explode. He moved between her legs, took a finger and inserted it into her already wet and throbbing pussy. He could feel her pussy tighten around his finger. Slowly, he pushed his finger farther in, teasing her; when he thought that she was ready he pulled his finger out and teased her with his cock. He loved how she reacted when he touched her. Then he took his large cock and slowly inserted it into her, making sure he did not hurt her.

Once he knew that she was comfortable, he began to speed up. Shortly thereafter, he got to see Bailey's wild side. She began to arch her body to meet his pace. Then she ran her nails over his body, feeling how he shivered. She knew she was getting to him by the way his erection jumped and twitched at her touch.

Her eyes were focused on him; Draven could see how much she loved him, it was written in her eyes. It was one of the things that set her apart; he could see the love on her face. With other women he had always been able to see when they weren't honest with him, or in love with him for that matter. Other women used him for his power and money. But he knew he did not have to worry about Bailey being dishonest or ingenuous.

Draven kissed her eyelids as he felt his climax getting closer and closer. "I love you, Bailey Marie. Forever and always."

Shocked at what he'd said, she stopped. "You do?" Sweat glistened over his body; she knew he was close to climax.

Bailey pushed at his chest until he shifted back, and then she climbed on top of him, taking her time and grinding on his cock. Staring into his deep green eyes, she was almost getting lost in what she was doing.

She could not believe that he had just told her that; she thought that she was dreaming. It was nice to know that he felt the same way about her as she did him. As she continued to ride him, she began to run her hands over his chest, kissing every little inch on him. Bailey was so close to climaxing, but she wanted to make sure that Draven reached his before she did. She wanted him to be fully sated and content.

She realized as she was just about to make him cum that he had never put a condom on. Stopping dead mid-thrust, she looked at him with a smirk. "You forgot something, dear."

Draven knew exactly what she was referring to. He did not say a word.

He began arching into her and caressing her full and perky breasts, pulling at them as he pumped his cock harder into her. "Bailey, if you want to know what it is like to be one of my kinds, I will show you."

Before she knew it she was on her hands and knees and Draven was behind her, pounding his thick erection into her. He began rubbing and slapping her ass as he pushed into her.

"Mm mm, baby. Show me how bad you want it, take it all," she was gasping. God, he was bigger now than ever before. She thought it would hurt. To her surprise, it did not hurt at all; it actually turned her on more. Bailey was not usually one for rough sex, but this was incredible. She felt things that she never had before and she loved it. A moan slipped from her mouth and she rose up to her knees wrapping one arm around his neck.

"I love you, Draven. More than you will ever know."

He knew that she was the one that he wanted by his side. Wrapping his hands in her long, curly red hair, he pounded faster into her until he climaxed. He did not move away as he usually did when they had sex. He stayed tight behind her, holding her body against his. It felt almost ritualized.

Bailey awakened to Draven's hard cock against her back with soft kisses to her neck and shoulders. She felt his skilled fingers as they worked her clit while she turned and moaned into the crook of his neck. Though it seemed like they'd just fucked, she wanted more because she missed him so much.

Still wet from their earlier fuck, Bailey placed her hand on top his as he inserted a finger into her and increased the pressure on her hot wet pussy. She loved the sensation and wanted to feel Draven's thick erection inside her again. It made her pussy wetter at the thought.

Before she could reach behind her to grab his hard dick that felt like steel against her ass, Driven forced Bailey on her back and rolled on top her.

"I can't ever get enough of you", Draven whispered as he peered with love into her eyes and kissed her lips softly. Her pussy dripped at the sensation of his kisses and scent, she was overwhelmed with need. "I thought about fucking you every day I was away from you."

"Please fuck me", Bailey begged as she grabbed his shoulders and pulled him down for a kiss.

"Tell me how much you missed me baby, how much you've missed feeling my hard cock inside you." Draven grunted as he broke the kiss, sat up and pulled her body in position to enter her fast and hard.

She felt his long thick rod against her stomach as he wrapped her legs around his waist.

"I missed all of you." Bailey breathed as Draven guided his erection to her wet cunt and filled her to the hilt. He groaned as he felt her hot heat engulf his cock and pulled out of her slow only enter her again harder with force.

He leaned down and sucked her breast into his mouth as he started to pound into her harder each time. She needed this, they needed this and she couldn't have been happier for a better homecoming.

The moans and the sound of their wet skin slapped as he grinded and pounded relentlessly was too much for Bailey to bear. She felt the buildup and it didn't' take much longer for her to cum hard as she yelled Draven's name. She held on to him tighter and her nails dug into his back as he hammered her pussy harder and harder.

She milked his cock over and over as she came while Draven continued to drill her cunt like a piston.

"Cum inside me!" Bailey pleaded. With

that request, Draven, grunted as he released into her and pumped all he had to give inside her.

Their heavy breathing filled the room as they both came down from their highs. Draven pulled out as cock softened, spent from the need for a round two and show her how much he needed her. He pulled them to their sides with her back to his front and whispered, "I can't wait for round three."

She wondered briefly if there was a reason for it, but for now she was too exhausted to ask. All she really cared about was the fact that he was home and he said that he loved her. With that she closed her eyes and grinded her back against him, quickly falling fast asleep.

2 SHOW ME HOW BAD YOU WANT IT

The next morning Bailey woke up delightfully sore after last night's excursion. Her body was still intertwined with Draven's massive, naked limbs. She watched him sleeping; he really did look so peaceful. She thought she could stay that way forever.

He had said that he loved her. Bailey was elated, but still she was not sure whether he had really meant it. Could it have been a ploy to get her into bed with him? That was unlikely, given that she'd already been ready to give herself to him. Maybe it had just come out in the heat of the moment, but he hadn't really meant it? She tried not to think about it.

Smiling, she thought over the night

before. The taste of his skin. His hands on her hips, grinding her into him. The smell of sweat heavy in the air. The feeling of his big cock inside her. Bailey relived those moments, squirming against Draven's heavy body. The softness of her skin rubbing against him provoked a response from his own body. She felt his cock growing hard, digging into her lower back and between her ass. She pushed back a bit, and he groaned.

Impish ideas began to run through Bailey's mind. One hand trailed down her neck, brushing over her breast and grazing her nipple. She gasped, then moaned. Before she knew, her other hand was running down her stomach, playing with the soft flesh of her groin. She began to squirm as one finger slipped into her core. It was warm and wet, and blissful. She was writhing against Draven's body, grinding against his rock-hard cock. She wanted him again badly.

Bailey was so lost in herself, she didn't notice when Draven woke up. Suddenly his hands were on her, cupping her breasts. He pinched her nipples playfully, then moved his hand down to her hip and pulled her against him. His moans echoed in her ears.

"Mmm...good morning," he whispered.

"Hi," she giggled back, turning to face him.

He kissed her forehead, her cheeks, and down to her neck. She nibbled on his ear, sucked gently on his neck and shoulders. Then he rolled over on top of her, and slowly slid himself inside her. He kissed her neck and down to her breasts as he started a slow torturous movement as to tease her.

Bailey's head rolled back as she felt his massive cock moving within her. As Draven began to slowly pull himself out, her muscles clenched around him. As he pushed back in, she moaned. Wordlessly, he started moving faster.

Underneath him, Bailey writhed in pleasure. Her fingernails dug into his shoulders, urging him to go faster. She wrapped her legs around his hips, pulling him into her deeper with every thrust.

Their breathing began to pickup and a soft sheen of sweat formed between them as their pace quickened. The sound of their bodies slapping as Draven pounded her pussy hard was a definitely a morning ritual Bailey could get used to. His cock was enormous as he stretched her pussy and grinded deep inside her. She could feel him fill her so completely. Even though her pussy was still wore out from the night before, she loved him and would stay in bed and fuck him all day if that was what he desired.

Bailey could feel an orgasm welling up

inside of her. All the muscles in his body tensed in anticipation. Draven noticed; he began pushing harder, faster. She cried out, a long, high moan, as waves of pleasure rolled through her body. Draven gasped, pulled out quickly, and shot his thick stream onto her stomach and breasts. She almost wanted to protest that he didn't come inside again like the night before.

He collapsed beside her, panting. She curled up in the hollow of his body, reveling in the warmth of his skin. Soon, she was asleep again. He was just starting to drift off with her, when the quiet buzzing of his phone roused him. He rolled over to answer it.

"Alverez is in a secure location, sir. We will find out what his plans are and we will let you know."

Closing his eyes, Draven sighed a deep sigh of relief. Their mission had gone well, but transport could be tricky. It was good to know that Bastion Alverez was no longer a threat. "Thanks, Lenex. I will be there in a little bit. I need to take care of some personal business first before I come down to HQ." With that he hung up the phone.

Now, back to more important things. He rolled over, kissing Bailey's bare shoulder. Her skin was so soft; he loved every inch of it all the way down to the angel kiss that she had on her inner thigh. He gently wrapped his arm around her body, careful not to wake her.

He never thought that she would see his other side, the side he hid from the rest of the world, and accept him for what and who he was. It was truly a gift to have her at his side. The one thing that he wondered was what she would think if she were to become what he was. Only time would tell if she would actually go through with it and stick with him.

He got out of bed slowly, trying not to wake Bailey. He knew that she did not like waking up in an empty bed. She understood he only left when he had to, but it didn't make it any easier to leave her in the morning. Especially when she had just poured her heart out to him the night before. He would have to make it back quickly so that she would not worry about him. That was one of the things he loved about her. It did not matter how long he was gone, when he arrived back home, he knew that she would be happy to see him. He knew that Bailey was truly one of a kind; he hoped that she would keep her promise to stay with him forever.

When Bailey awoke and realized that she was alone in Draven's bed, she was saddened; she had hoped that she would wake up in his arms. She knew that he probably had details to finish up from the last mission. He would be back as soon as he could.

Although she didn't know much about his job, she knew that it could be dangerous. It was enough to make her worry – what would happen if he was injured, or worse, killed, on a job? She promised herself that she was not going to think about that. She needed to get up and go for a run.

As she jumped out of bed, she noticed that she felt different this morning. She was more at peace, more content, but it was more than that. She had never felt so strong. She felt a protectiveness and love for Draven that she had not felt so strongly before. Why did she feel this way now?

Smiling, she pulled her purple running pants out of the dresser and grabbed a black tank top out of the closet. She wanted to wear something that was loose and wouldn't touch her skin too much. Something was not right, but she couldn't put her finger on it. It was almost as if her skin was on fire. She tried not to think about it; after all, she had just woken up. Bailey grabbed her running shoes from next to the big mansion door, slipping them on she took off down the path into the woods.

As Draven arrived at his office, he saw Lenex Gafton sitting in the big chair behind his desk, with his feet up the desk and his eyes closed. It was not until Draven opened the door to the office that he moved.

"How is Mr. Alverez this morning?" Lenex moved out of his chair and Draven sat at his desk, looking over the notes from the night before. He was puzzled; it almost seemed that Alverez wanted to get caught. Things had been too easy. He hadn't really put up a fight. The question was, why?

"Can anyone tell me why he came so peacefully? It seems suspicious to me that a big guy like him doesn't fight the arrest at all?"

Lenex nodded at Draven as he sat in the leather chair on the other side of Draven's desk. "Maybe he's taking the fall for someone higher up the chain? Given his past work with other drug lords, it is a possibility. Or maybe he let us take him, but I don't know why. I guess for now all we can do is pay close attention and hope that we are wrong. But until we find out more, I'll keep the team on alert."

Until this mission was put to rest, not

only he was in danger, but so was Bailey. And she didn't even know what was happening. How could she hope to protect herself?

He thanked Lenex for all of his hard work, reiterating that Alverez must not escape from his cell. Now he had to make sure that Bailey was safe and would remain safe until this mission was over.

It seemed to take forever for Draven to get home. When he reached home everything looked fine. As he opened the door, he called her name. When she did not answer or come to meet him, he became worried. Had something happened to her? Was she freaked out after last night's revelations? It was hard to tell. He just wanted to know that she was safe. He would not rest until she was in his arms. He had made a promise to her that he would always keep her safe, and he was going to make sure that he lived up to his word.

As Bailey crossed the small creek in the woods, she noticed how the sun was playing off the water. It was truly beautiful, like the creek had diamonds flowing in its waters. It was one the many reasons that she liked to run in the morning.

Plus, she loved to see Draven drool when she returned, glistening with sweat. It really seemed to turn him on. It usually led to many hours of fucking which neither could get enough of. She smiled mischievously as she ran.

She stopped for a moment to catch her breath and look all around her. She began to feel as if someone or something was watching her, but she couldn't find a reason for it. She was starting to wish that she had not decided to go running. God, what she would have given to have Draven there with her. Bailey began to long for Draven's strong arms around her.

Draven shifted quickly into his jaguar form, trying to cover more ground in his search. He could feel her heart racing and he could tell that she was becoming more and more frightened by the moment. He wished he had revealed himself to her sooner, had explained how dangerous it could be to be with him. Draven only hoped that it had nothing to do with Alverez. He had to get to her quick.

Spinning around and around, Bailey could not tell what was scaring her. All she knew was that she felt like someone's prey, that they were toying with her and she did not like it. She decided to climb into one of the trees so she could see anyone around her. She hoped that whatever was watching her would not be able to come up after her. She had a strange feeling that it was not going to really matter, but she had to make some attempt.

From the high tree branches, she could see it clearly – moving slowly through the thick carpet of ferns was a young, white tiger. No, not moving – stalking. She gasped as it locked its eyes on her. It began moving toward her tree, and Bailey realized she had no place to run, now.

Suddenly, a black jaguar burst through the brush and tore down the path toward the tiger. Bailey watched wide-eyed as Draven chased down the tiger and pounced on it. He pinned the other cat to the ground, gripping its neck tightly in his jaws. He gave a warning growl and a little snarl before releasing the other cat. The tiger took off.

Not sure what was happening, Bailey stayed silent until he shifted back to his human form, only to notice that he was naked.

God, his muscles were so defined and gleaming with sweat. She wondered how he had found her. She hadn't left a note because she thought that she would be home before he was. Was that one of the many things she did not know about him? She scampered quickly down the tree.

From a thick branch about ten feet

above Draven's head, she jumped down to land next to him, landing solidly on her feet. She didn't really think about; she was just happy to have Draven by her side.

Holding her close to him, he checked her over to make sure that she was not hurt in any way. It took all that he had to keep cool and not seem more worried than he normally would be. He had to find the best way to tell her that until his mission was done, she had to be more careful. He didn't want to scare her, and there was so much she didn't know. The question was how to tell her in a way that would not drive her away from him; he really did not want to risk losing her.

Draven held her for a few moments to make sure that she was okay. Her heart rate slowly returned to normal.

"I am sorry you were scared by the tiger, I should have said something to you. They are not common here, but every once in a while in this area you will see one or two. You need to keep yourself safe. Anytime you are going to be running, please just let me know. So I can protect you whenever you need me to. After all, you are my mate."

There was something different about Draven and the way that he was acting; it was almost like he had an animalistic impulse to protect her. All she wanted to do right then was make love to him. The way his arms wrapped around her as he held her against his muscular frame made her skin tingle. Every little thing made her want him more.

Bailey began kissing his chest, gently nipping at his taunt flesh. She looked up at him with a mischievous smirk; Draven could only smile, somewhat sheepishly, in response. She led him into the trees away from prying eyes. Dropping to her knees on the moss-covered ground, she ran her hands over his stomach all the way down to his already hard cock. She gently stroked his cock, and began to run her tongue softly up and down his length.

He looked down at her with his eyes full of passion and desire. God, she looked so beautiful. Her eyes were the brightest green that he had ever seen. It was as if she was full of life that he had never noticed before. She really took his breath away; he had to have her. But not like this, not right now. It wasn't safe here. He wanted to get her up the house.

Bailey had other ideas. When he tried to pull away, she began sucking harder. When he rested his hands on her shoulders, trying to pull her back, she began tracing her fingers over the sensitive skin of his balls. With her soft lips wrapped around his cock, Draven was powerless. His knees began to tremble, threatening to give out.

With one hand, Bailey massaged his cock as she sucked on the tip. With the other, she ran her fingernails up from his groin to his stomach, then around over his hip to his back. She reached up as high as she could before trailing them down to his buttocks, playfully squeezing. Then down the back of his thigh, lightly tickling the space behind his knee, and down his calf, before coming back up to graze the inside of his thigh.

Draven groaned, his member throbbing for release. He forgot all about the tiger, his enemies, and the mission. He was powerless as Bailey teased and toyed with his cock. She ran the tip of her tongue from the tip of his cock to the base, and then drew tiny circles with it as she moved back up its length. He gasped as she nibbled gently while she stroked his balls.

Bailey began to moan. His skin was glistening and salty with sweat. He tasted so good as she wrapped her lips around his substantial girth. His cock was huge, but she greedily took it into her mouth, feeling it slide into the back of her throat.

Draven grabbed a fistful of her hair, pulling hard. She responded by sucking on his cock, deep, hard sucks. He gasped, and his hands moved to her shoulders. His fingers dug into her shoulders as his weight bore down on her.

He was close, she knew it. Bailey moved

both hands to his cock, gripping the shaft hard as she sucked and licked at the head. His groans grew louder, his grip harder on her shoulders.

"Oh, God," he groaned, just as he shot a stream of cum down her throat. Bailey swallowed, greedily licking the tip of his cock, milking the last drop.

Draven looked down at her, seeing her mischievous smile as she licked her lips. Now, she was in trouble.

He shape shifted into the jaguar, laid on the ground and waited until she climbed on his back. When he knew that she had a strong grip, he took off straight for the house.

They made it back home safely from the run; however Bailey was only getting started. After Draven shifted back into human form, he was already naked. She would always get aroused when she saw a naked Draven before her, especially with his hard cock waiting to fill either her mouth or pussy. She missed him so much and having him home now, she knew she'd never get her fill of him.

"I missed you today." Bailey leaned up and kissed his lips softly. "I need you again, please."

"How bad do you want it baby?" He

grinned and nipped slowly across her neck.

"I can show you how bad." Bailey shot back with her most seductive smile.

Draven's eyes softened, he was holding back so much with Bailey and would have taken her earlier, but he'd been patient, and wanted to get her home first. There was still so much for her to learn about his kind and mating outdoors was not out of the ordinary.

"Take a shower with me," he whispered against her lips, brushing her hair back to see her face. Without hesitation, she placed her hand in his.

Slowly, he led her into the bathroom and turned on the shower. As the bathroom began to steam, he slowly undressed Bailey. He kissed her neck, eyes and lips softly, while slowly moving down to cup her breasts.

He took turns taking each one of her hard nipples into his mouth. He licked and sucked slowly, loving each one slowly and making Bailey wetter and needier for him. Bailey groaned at the sensations his tongue was giving her and her sounds made his cock harder. He quickly lifted her up to carry her into the shower as the hot steamy water cascaded around them.

Draven backed her into the wall and quickly dropped to his knees. He threw Bailey's leg over his shoulder and without warning, thrust his tongue inside her hot pussy. His tongue was fast and needy biting and licking her clit. She writhed against the wall with her head thrashing from side to side moaning his name. She grabbed his hair forcefully as leverage to grind her pussy against his tongue as he continued to fuck her pussy with his mouth.

It seemed like hours and orgasms later before Draven was done giving her pleasure. He looked up at her and with one last lick to her pussy, the need to be inside her. He stood wrapping her arms around his neck and he kneeling to pick Bailey up by her waist, this time his back against the wall.

Bailey took Draven's face between her hands and looked into his eyes, the unspoken love evident between them. His cock bounced against her pussy, grinding and awaiting for permission to enter. "Love me." she whispered against his lips.

"Always baby," his whispered back taking her tongue deeply into his mouth. He closed his eyes and grasped her hips tightly. He slowly guided his rock hard cock into her wet pussy, deepening their kiss. They both moaned at the sensation as his hands wrapped around her hips tighter to hold her in place against him. Bailey threw her head back as Draven started to pump his cock into her faster.

The warm water cascading down on them and the hard thrusts as her back bounced against the shower wall over and over again was almost too much to endure.

Draven looked down between them as his cock pumped in and out of Bailey." See baby, this is home. You are my mate." She loved when he made declarations that they belonged together. Hearing his words and feeling his body move deep inside her sparked feelings unfamiliar to her. She continued to meet his every thrust, warning him that she was going to come again.

Bailey could feel his cock swelling inside her pussy. She tightened her grip on his shoulders and she started to come." I love you Draven." He pumped harder as she started to milk his cock. With one last hard thrust, he held her tightly to him and pumped his seed into her trembling and gasping for breath.

"I love you too Bailey." He whispered into her ear.

Tonight would be a night that she would never forget. If she was willing, he would take the next step to making her more like him.

3 THE MATING BEGINS

Bailey's body was warm to the touch even after just getting out of a cool shower. Draven and Baley's need for each other was so powerful, that they continued another round of lovemaking in the bedroom. With both of their bodies still damp from the shower, the feeling was even more sensual as they explored each once again.

Draven easily slid inside her wet pussy, pumping slowly in and out basking in the feeling of being so deep inside her. She clawed at his back, wanting him to speed up his movements. He sat back on his knees and grabbed her hips tightly guiding her fast and hard onto his cock like a piston. Bailey cried out once again as her orgasm took over, clearly tired from their sex marathon.

He finally came hard one last time hoping their love and sex life continued to get better. He loved being able to open up to Bailey, to express his love both physically and emotionally.

Draven knew that he had to finish the transformation soon or she was going to be in an immense amount of pain and he did not want that for her. He wanted her transformation to go as smoothly as possible.

He also knew he would have to stay close and protect her from any other males who might pick up the scent of the powerful pheromones her body would be producing. Even with their boss in holdings, Alverez's men would likely try to get to her during this tumultuous time, but he would not let that happen. She was his mate. For the first time in his life, Draven felt truly connected to someone and he was not going to let anything happen to her. He even considered calling Lenex in for some backup, if the need arose.

As he lay next to her while she rested, Draven knew that he was going to have to be gentle over the next few days. She was going to be on edge and her body would be on fire. But the only thing that would help the fire fade was his touch, so he was going to have to be with her 24 hours a day until she was fully turned.

It was not often that a dominate male would find his female so early in life; he was only 28 years old. Sometimes, people thought he was much younger, which occasionally worked to his advantage. Most of the time, it was a pain in the ass, especially when he wanted to go for a Jack and Coke after a mission and the bar refused to serve him. Lately it was less of an issue; he rarely went for a drink anymore after a mission, as he was always excited to get home to Bailey.

It was so nice to have her in his life; he needed her more than he thought he would. She was what was missing from his life in the military. There was just something about her that made everything perfect. As she lay on the bed, he curled his body around hers, trying to calm the jerky twitching of her changing muscles.

Draven knew that after the jerky muscles, next came soaring body temperatures and the craziness would really start. He had to be ready to help her, especially when it came to her sexual desires. It would be a long night; the females of his species already had a high sex drive, but when they were in the middle of the transformation it became practically insatiable. It could be dangerous for the male if he denied her. It was not unheard of for a female to become violent, even to the point of killing her mate if she is rebuked. That is why he had to make sure that he was able to get enough rest and food in this lull; once she awoke, there would be no rest for him.

Before he closed his eyes to sleep, he ran his hands through her hair. He could not believe that this was happening to him; it all seemed like a dream. Bailey had given him so much in the short time that they had been together; he was glad that she was going to be his forever. With that he closed his eyes and drifted off to sleep.

When Draven woke, he found himself alone in bed. Where was Bailey?

He threw on his robe and ran downstairs, hoping that she had not decided to go for another run. He found her in his study, sitting next to the fireplace in a high-backed chair, reading a book, "What to Know About Your Transformation into the Trigarian World." How did she know where to find that book?

She looked up at him, kind of puzzled.

"Is this what you are, Draven?" She continued to look through the book.

Walking over, he knelt down next to her, looking up into her sparkling eyes. "Yes, love, this is what I am. But this book does not tell you that every case of transformation is, umm..., different in its own way. There are some who are born Trigarian, and then there are others who are introduced into the world. Sometimes someone might find out by accident what they are, because their parents never told them."

She looked up at him, her brow furrowed in worry. "I had a dream about this book. In my dream, it showed me right where it was in here. I had to read a little bit of it if I were to become like you. In some ways I think I am already showing signs of becoming like you. Is that possible?"

Looking into her eyes, he saw more curiosity than fear. "Yes, it is possible, although it is very rare. In my family it has only happened one other time." He could tell Bailey was beginning to get scared. She quickly got up and ran to the bathroom.

'Uh, oh,' Draven thought. 'Here we go.'

Again, he thought about calling his team in to patrol the property's perimeter and make sure that she was kept safe during her transformation.

He ran up to the bathroom to check on Bailey. When he got there, he found her passed out on the tile floor. He scooped her up in his arms. "Bailey, love, come on, come back to me. Stay with me, come on,

I'm right here. I will be with you. I will help you get through this." Placing her on their bed, he quickly called Lenex.

"Hey, I need you and the guys to come to my place. Bailey is going through her transformation and I need some reinforcements ASAP." With that he hung up and began to strip her of her running suit. Anything she wore during the transformation would be ruined.

Her body was becoming hotter to the touch. He offered her a glass of water from the bedside table, hoping that she would take a sip. He did not want her to become dehydrated. Once she took a sip, he held her and used a wash cloth to wipe her body down, trying to cool her off a little more.

Twenty minutes had passed and the men had arrived at Draven's home. As they walked in, Lenex called up to Draven to let him know that they were there. Draven came down to meet them and to let them know why they had been called to his home. They all knew that they had to be at the top of their game. It was nice to see the six of them again; he just wished that it had been under better circumstances.

Geoff and Darian were standing up

against the wall, waiting to find out what their orders were. Those two never smiled, they never joked, no matter what the situation. While Draven sometimes wished they would lighten up, he never worried about the mission with these two – there would be no loopholes, no slip-ups with Geoff and Darian around.

Then there was Ty and Landon, the twins. They were standing at the end of the stairs, looking up at Draven. Even after all this time working together, the only way he could tell the difference was the falcon tattoo – each twin had the same tattoo, but they were on opposite arms.

Then finally, Michael and Skyler, his stealth soldiers. Draven knew that at night, they would be put on guard. When it came to stealth missions, Michael and Skyler were the best.

Each and every one of the men knew that when Draven called them together it was something important. After telling the men what was happening with Bailey and that Alverez's men were in the area, they all knew what they needed to do. It was up to them to guard the mansion until Bailey's transformation was complete. If one of Alverez's men got into the home, Bailey could be killed. None of them wanted that. With their orders explained, the men dispersed.

Now Draven could concentrate on

Bailey and make sure that her crossing over went smoothly.

Draven went back upstairs to find Bailey on the bed on her knees, playing with her breasts and flicking them with her tongue. God, did that turn him on. He grinned mischievously. She craved him; it was about time for the first round of mating to begin. He could smell the powerful pheromones she was giving off. Draven had never smelled anything so amazing. As he walked over to her, throwing his robe to the other side of the room, she gave him a devilish smirk. He knew what she needed and he was going to give it to her as long as she wanted it.

Crawling up on the bed next to Bailey, he began kissing her neck and running his hands over her body. She needed him. She needed release. Now.

Starting out slowly, he began by playing with her pussy, dipping two fingers in and quickly pulling them out, teasing her. Then he laid her down on her back, careful not to make her wait too long. Draven began to go down on her, teasing her pussy with his tongue until she began to grind her hips against him. He loved how her body reacted, so natural and fluid with his.

His cock was already rock hard and wanted release so bad that it began to throb. Without thinking, he stopped and spread her legs apart so that he could look at all of her. Every inch of her was beautiful and he was going to make sure that every little inch of her body was satisfied. But before he could continue she had switched positions, and now she was sucking on his cock and her pussy was in his face. It was not what he'd planned, but he went along with it and let her call the shots.

Slowly, she began sucking on his cock, letting her hands wander all over his body. She knew that he was the one that she wanted; there could be no one else. But she didn't understand why she suddenly needed him like this. Usually she could pace herself; today it was like an all-consuming fire that only his touch or kisses could put out. When he was pleasing her, she had orgasm after orgasm. She could feel another orgasm starting to form in her core. What was going on?

Draven could feel another orgasm building up. He could not help himself; he reached for her ample breasts and played with them as he continued to nibble on her pussy.

Her body started to arch in response to Draven's touch. Pulling his head up, he watched her reaction. He knew that soon she would be begging for him to make love to her and that was the moment he could not wait for.

Without even asking, he again placed himself between her legs and started teasing her swollen pussy with his rock hard cock. It wasn't until she started to arch uncontrollably that he realized that he may have waited a little too long for her. Without hesitation he drove his cock into her and as he began to get faster and faster she met his pace. He could see desperation in her eyes. He knew that from then on they were connected as one; she was going to be his mate for life.

Carefully he lifted her legs up around his neck so he could drive his cock into her deeper. Without warning, she came all over his cock. She was not done, though; she began to run her hands through his long black hair, pulling at it as if to let him know that she not only wanted to play more , but she wanted it rougher . Draven smiled; it was his job to make sure that all of her wants and needs were filled, and he was happy to oblige.

Pulling her up to her knees, he began to pull her hair lightly. Out of nowhere there was a mixture of a moan and a growl at the same time. When that happened he knew that the female jaguar was close and wanted to be released; he also knew that if he rushed the process, Bailey would be hurt. He was careful not to push the animal inside out just yet...

4 HIDDEN DESIRE INSIDE

Although the thought that the female jaguar was begging for release excited Draven in more than one way, he knew that if he rushed things, it was more than likely that both Bailey and the jaguar would end up getting hurt. With that in mind, Draven let go of her hair and began to kiss her lower back, running his rough, calloused hands all over her body. He knew that she wanted it a little rougher, but he also knew that there were some risks he wasn't willing to take. Still, Bailey made it so hard to resist her.

Suddenly she was backing up, thrusting against his cock. He could not believe it - she was actually mating with him. Animalistic desire and instincts took over her. As her body began to undulate faster on his cock, he knew beyond a shadow of a doubt that she had wanted to go through with it – she was going to mate with him no matter what. Her pussy clamped down on his cock as he came, milking him of all of his precious seed.

Draven knew that at this point he had better not move; if he did, there was a chance of hurting her. She had given herself to him with no fight, and he'd known how much he meant to her then. She meant so much more to him now. She was his and would be his for a life time.

But he also knew that the mating was not yet finished. Bailey was going to need him again soon, but until then he needed to calm her down and get her to rest. This was the first wave of the transformation; it would only get more intense until she was fully turned.

Then he was going to have to teach her what it really meant to be a Trigarian. But that would come later; for now, he needed to get her to lie down and rest. He slowly pulled himself out of her as her muscles relaxed, and then he motioned for her to lie down next to him. From here on out, she was his responsibility; there was no going back, he had found his mate for life. Carefully, he wrapped his body around hers as she closed her eyes and fell into a restful sleep.

Before he knew it there was a pounding on the bedroom door. Before it could wake Bailey, Draven jumped out of bed with lightning quick speed and opened the door, not caring that he was stark naked. Lenex was at the door looking at him with a bit of panic on his face, but he waited until Draven has closed the door quietly before speaking. He knew that female jaguars tend to get cranky when they are woken.

"What is it, Lenex?"

"Alverez escaped. He and his men ransacked HQ."

Draven became worried – with Bailey in mid-transformation, if he were to leave her she could come to resent him and refuse to finish the mating. Then they could never be a whole as his kind was meant to be; that could not only lead to a lot of heartache and pain, but possibly death if things went very badly.

'God, could things just not be so complicated for once?' Draven thought.

Lenex then grinned and chuckled. "Sir, if I may say, anytime that you have a woman around there tends to be more trouble than you can handle."

Draven growled a warning to Lenex that he had over-stepped his bounds. "You may think that now, young one, but the thing that you do not realize is how precious the women are to our kind."

He directed Lenex to take the twins, Michael and Skyler to find Alverez and kill him. Draven did not have the time or the patience to deal with assholes like Alverez right then. He had other things that required his full attention. With that he went back into the bedroom and closed the door behind him.

Draven knew he had to protect Bailey at all costs; if Alverez or his boss found out that Bailey was his mate, they would come after her to gain control over the Trigarians. He was not going to let that happen. Bailey was his and he would protect what was his at any cost.

He climbed into bed next to her, slightly touching her forehead to see if she had a fever. To his surprise, her skin was cool and dry. This was a good thing; it meant that he still had some time to rest until the next wave of passion hit and Bailey would need him again.

Lenex took the men to find Alverez, hoping to discover what, if anything, they had taken from headquarters. He knew that if Alverez found any information on the Trigarians, they would be hunted to the last living member. If he knew the location of the Trigarian elders, that would almost as bad. Without leadership, the

Trigarians would easily fall to their enemies.

He could not afford to mess up this mission, an entire species rested on his shoulders.

And the mission would be that much harder because Alverez would know they were coming for him. There would be no surprise in the attack this time.

Back at the mansion, Bailey had been sleeping for three hours. Draven was glad that her body was adjusting well to the change. He had known some members of the clan who died trying to save their mate during the transformation, all because their bodies could not handle the change. The mates would burn up with fever so high it would eventually kill them. But he knew that Bailey would make it, as long as they got through this part of the transformation.

As he looked at her sleeping so peacefully he wondered why it took him so long to find her. She was truly a beautiful creature. Her curly red locks flowed around her face. Her piercing green eyes took his breath away. For most Trigarians, that would have been enough. But Bailey was smart, and Draven loved that the most about her. She was extremely smart. There was something about her thought process, how she figured things out, it just made him love her more.

Out of nowhere, Bailey sat up in bed. Draven was halfway across the room, looking out the window. He could tell that she was looking for him just by the scent of her pheromones. God, he didn't think he would ever get enough of that smell.

As he turned toward her, he heard a low wanton moan come out of Bailey as she climbed out of bed and walked seductively over to him, swaying her hips. Dropping to her knees, she took his already erect cock into her mouth, swirling her tongue around the tip of his cock.

Damn, she was good. She knew what really drove him to the edge of almost exploding in her mouth. As she looked up at him with desire in her eyes, he could see that the jaguar in her was begging and pleading to be pleased by him. Pulling her up to her feet, he began kissing her neck, nipping at it once in a while, letting the jaguar know that he knew what she needed and he was willing to please her in any way he could. Bailey moaned at the touch of Draven's mouth on her breasts as he went down, kissing her stomach before sliding two of his fingers inside of her. It was a white hot, moist feeling that he loved. Her muscles were expanding and contracting on his fingers as he pulled them out and inserted them repeatedly. In between, he licked them clean.

As he continued to pleasure her both

inside and out he watched every emotion that washed over her body. He could feel her getting closer and closer to climaxing, but before she did he had to do one last thing to push her over the edge. He walked her over and sat her down at the edge of the bed, dropping down to his knees. He laid her back before beginning to play with her clit again, massaging it with his fingers and then taking her swollen pussy in his mouth. He loved how her body began to twitch when he touched her. She tasted so good to him; it was as if he could never get enough of her.

Without warning, she climaxed in his mouth.

Slapping her thigh gently, Bailey began to move her way up the bed. She knew by the mischievous look in his eyes that he was far from being done with her. And she wanted him again and again. He was the only one who could put out the fire that was raging through her body.

Draven knew he needed to mate with Bailey soon, as she was beginning to feel too hot. He gently climbed up between her legs, lifting them up slightly so he could bury his shaft deeper. He liked that she let him take the lead and do what he wanted with her.

When he made love to her, it was about more than just the act itself; he wanted to show her that he was giving her all of himself, including his heart and soul. For Trigarians, this was just one of the many ways that males showed their mates they were committed to only them and no other female.

Carefully, he teased her pussy with his cock. As she gasped, he quickly buried himself in her, rocking slowly back and forth. She moaned, arching her body to give him better access. Bailey felt so good to him, especially now that she was his; he knew now that no matter what she would be there when he needed her. A slightly high-pitched moan escaped Bailey's throat and he knew that she craved every inch of him. Her body met his beat for beat.

Suddenly her moans became a yowl, the call of a female panther in heat. He knew that this would be somewhat painful for her, but also one of the most exhilarating times she would have as his mate. He held on to her, pounding his overly large cock into her, hoping she did not get hurt. When the jaguar in his clan were close to orgasm, their erections became larger than normal; when they mated, it would actually almost hook into the female until the male had finished the mating. Although it was one of the roughest times for couples, it was also one of the most intense and sensual, especially for couples that were new to the clan.

As he continued, he could feel Bailey's

insides changing slowly. Once the process had started, he knew that the next time they would mate it would be as jaguars. She was not going to be an easy one to mate with that way; he would really have to be rough with her. He could feel the power that she possessed in her animal form.

He looked down at her beautiful, rosy red cheeks, her cream-colored skin and those bright green eyes that sparkled when he looked at her. "I love you, Bailey Marie, forever and always. And I pledge my heart and soul to you. You are my mate for life."

This time Bailey knew without doubt that he really did love her and only wanted her. But she also knew that this was not done. All that she knew now was there was looking back now; she was not the same person she had been just a few hours ago, and that did not bother her at all. She had Draven, and that was all she needed. With that she began to reach up to him and she kissed him, whispering in his ear. "I have loved you from day one, no matter what or who you are. You are my lover and my life, this I pledge to you, my love."

Draven was touched by the words that she spoke, and the knowledge that she did not regret what was being done to her. With that, he climaxed again inside of her.

Afterward, he kissed her forehead and whispered to her, "Now go to sleep and get some rest while you can. You are going to need all of the strength you can muster for the last part of the transformation."

With a small smile, Bailey curled up into a ball, and fell fast asleep.

He knew the next time that she woke he would have a new reason to live and love; she would be bound to him for life. Now all he had to do was make sure Alverez did not find out that she was his mate quite yet. It was difficult to hide though; the smell of pheromones permeated the air around them and the air outside. He knew that if Alverez and his men were anywhere nearby they would know right away. Alverez would try to take her for himself.

It was for that reason only that he would not leave her for one minute. Curling up around her, his body protected hers. He would stay with her, no matter what ...

Lenex could not understand how one man could escape from an HQ lockdown when so many others had tried and failed. Regardless, now they had to capture Alverez down again.

They had tracked him by scent back to the villa. It made sense, he guessed.

Where else would Alverez go, if not home? Still, something about it just did not feel right to him. It was too easy, too...simple.

As he peered across the courtyard at Alverez's villa, Lenex knew they would have to hit it harder and faster than last time. They had to make sure Alverez was taken care of, one way or another.

There was a sinking feeling in his gut that if he did not do this just right, one of them would not make it back. He and his men stayed in the high foliage of the jungle, careful to stay hidden as they monitored guard patrols and tried to locate Alverez. He was mulling ideas as he studied his enemies' movement. Whatever they decided on, this plan had to go off flawlessly. He knew if they wanted to pull this off, they needed to catch the guards at exactly the right moment.

Nightfall had come and the men continued to watch. Michael and Skyler had located Alverez moving about in his study on the west side of the villa. Alverez and his men were on high alert. Still, they needed a distraction to draw the guards away. But how?

Then it hit Skyler. "Let's use their nature against them. They are Pumarians, right? Aggressive, territorial, easily provoked? So let's pretend we're moving in on their turf. A new male in town, looking to expand his boundaries. They'll respond to a challenge like that, won't they? They're already all keyed up on high alert, all on edge and ready for a fight. So one of us leads them away. That still leaves two to take out the stragglers, and two more to go after Alverez. He won't have anyone there to protect him."

Lenex wondered if it would be enough to trick Bastian's men into leaving him defenseless. He wasn't sure, but it was the best plan they had.

Draven's men waited until silence fell over the jungle. As the sun set they would take action and see if their plan worked.

Draven woke up wondering how his men were doing. Usually they would check in with him once in a while, but he knew that they were going to have to be even more careful than they usually were. He hated not being there with them; it was his job to make sure that nothing happened.

Doubtless, his men understood that he had other things that needed to be delicately handled first. As he lay next to Bailey, he again wondered how such an incredible woman had come into his life and offered to be part of his world without any questions asked.

As she lay there next to him he ran his fingers through her long curly red hair. Then he noticed that she began to arch into his arm as if they were having sex in her sleep. God, she was truly amazing. The fluid movements as she continued to move her body up and down in her sleep told him that she was definitely having sex with him in her sleep; he found himself becoming aroused just watching her. He reached down absent-mindedly to stroke his half-mast dick. It responded readily, growing stiff and warm in his hands.

He watched her writhing, listened to her moans. Then something unexpected happened – a low purr come from Bailey's throat as she was sleeping. Draven stopped stroking himself and stared at her in shock.

He knew that the animal inside of her was calling out to him to be released. But he was not going to answer to her quite yet; he wanted to make sure that Bailey was fully rested before they finished the mating process.

The last step in the mating process was not only the most intense, but also the most dangerous part. He had to make sure he did not hurt her in any way because it would leave a lasting memory for the female and she could be hesitant to mate with him again. If that happened, Bailey would ultimately become a loner

Trigarian and would not want any male. So he had to make sure he was careful to be just rough enough that she was pleased by it, but not so rough that he hurt her. It could be a thin line to walk.

He carefully climbed out of bed, trying not to shift her body too much.

Draven had to get some food in his system soon; he felt drained from having to be with her during the transformation, although he knew it was going to be well worth it. Carefully closing the door, he walked to the spare bedroom down the hall where his extra robe was. Putting it on, he decided to go downstairs for a moment to check in with his guards.

He was met in the kitchen by Geoff and Darian. They were sitting at the island, bullshitting with one another when they saw Draven.

"Man, you look like shit, Drav. She must really be a strong one to please. Do you need any help with that?" Geoff chuffed when he walked in, no hint a smile on his face.

Draven just chuckled. "I don't think you could handle her. She doesn't take orders lying down."

"It's been 14 hours, not done yet?" Darian asked.

"No, not quite yet, that's why I came down here. Get something to eat and drink before I go back up there. She's sleeping now."

All of the sudden the sound of glass shattering came from upstairs. Without pause, the men broke into a dead run for the bedroom, with Draven leading the pack. His worst fear had happened. Alverez and his men were with his mate. He would not let them harm her. She was his and only his. He had to get in there before another male mated her.

5 A NEW BEGINNING

Draven broke down the door just as one of Alverez's men tried to jump on top of the bed where Bailey lay completely lifeless and naked. Draven knew that she was okay; she was still in a deep sleep and would not wake up for a bit, or one could hope. He would hate to see what she would be able to do as a Trigarian, but for now she was helpless.

Geoff and Darian, both already in jaguar form, snarled and hissed at the intruders. The Pumarians chuffed back, teeth bared, ears pinned to their heads.

Draven and his men surrounded the bed as one of Alverez's men tried to mount Bailey. The air was heavy with the pungent musk of males vying for dominance. The scent alone was enough to infuriate him – these men were in his home, with his mate. Draven snarled at them, though he maintained his human form.

It happened almost too fast for Draven to track. With one quick pounce, Geoff threw the male off the bed, pinned the male to the ground, and broke his neck with a sickening crack. Now there was only one left, but Draven didn't want him dead. He would be a valuable source of information, with proper motivation. Darian threw the Pumarian around the room like a rag doll until his head struck a wooden beam and he collapsed, unmoving, to the floor.

With a glance to Draven, Geoff slipped out the window to check the property for any other intruders. Meanwhile, Darian shifted back to human form and stood over the intruder. Draven nodded at him; he knew what to do. Darian slipped some restraints onto the unconscious man's wrists, and hauled the man to the basement, where Draven had an interrogation room built just for such an occasion.

Draven turned his attention to Bailey, checking her over to make sure she was unharmed. There was not a scratch on her, but now she was starting to stir. He thanked God that she had not woken up when the other men were there; she probably would have been really pissed off... or really turned on. Either way, it could have been bad. A female is heat could be violently angry, and almost irresistible to any male nearby when she wanted to be. He would rather not have to fight with his men; they were like family.

"Good morning, beautiful." Bailey blushed as she realized that she was still naked and wrapped up in the sheets. God, what time was it? Had she stayed in bed this whole time? She felt fidgety, like she was not quite comfortable in her own skin. She had dreamt that she was able to transform into a creature like Draven. It was disturbing, frightening and yet appealing, somehow.

She looked at Draven with puzzlement in her eyes. "Am I... What...? How?" She couldn't make herself actually ask him. Was she able to do these things, like he could? Or was that some fantasy that her mind had made up? She had to know.

Draven took her hand and pressed it against his heart. He could smell her fear mingling with her powerful pheromones. He knew all she wanted was for him to make love to her, to release the animal within her. One final mating and the transformation would be complete. There would be no more pain, no more anxiety – it would be just the two of them, forever.

Right now, though, he needed to calm

her down so that her heart would stop racing as it was. Whispering in her ear, he said something in another language that she did not quite understand. Whatever it was, though, it was beautiful and somehow calming; she wondered what other interesting and beautiful things she was going to learn if they were an item.

Her bright green eyes were filled with fear. "Love, there is nothing to fear. I will be right here to protect you and keep you safe," Draven assured her.

He could tell that she was not sure what was happening to her yet. Quickly shape shifting into the jaguar that she loved so much, he lay down beside her. He knew that she felt more at peace when the jaguar was with her. She reached out to stroke his smooth coat and then she noticed the scar above the left eye. She wondered how he managed to get it.

"It is alright, Draven. You can show yourself, I am okay now," she smiled at him.

He shifted back, stretching his long, naked body next to hers on the bed. "That scar above my eye is from a fight with one of the Pumarians. They are the enemy of our race. One of their leaders tried to harm someone in my clan and I killed them for it. Ever since, they have been trying to get back at me for it. But before we go any further there is something that we need to talk about." He ran his hands through her long red hair and started to whisper something in another language. It was truly beautiful; after he was done he noticed that she had completely calmed down. "Do you remember when you said you would do anything to be with me because you loved me? Well, there is something I don't think you understand. You will be able to transform into a Trigarian just as I am able to; not yet, but soon. I can smell it in the air. So can the other Trigarian males downstairs."

Bailey didn't know how she was supposed to react. He could have mentioned earlier that if she was with him and loved him that she would be able to turn into this amazing creature. It both scared and excited her.

"Bailey, love... the transformation is going to be painful. But it won't last long, and when it's over, we'll be together, forever. Know that while you go through this for me, I am going through this with you and will be there for you when you need me most."

He could feel her hesitation as soon as he mentioned pain. He looked into her emerald green eyes, trying to reassure her as best he could. He was going to shield her from as much of the pain as he could, but he knew that he could not take all of it away. Draven leaned in slowly and kissed her with more passion than ever before, hoping that it would get her mind off of what she was just told. He knew she was strong enough to go through it; he just needed her to know that.

Looking into his eyes, Bailey felt a rush of pride and honor that he chose her to be his mate above all others. She didn't understand exactly what she was getting herself into, but she had made the decision to be with him no matter what, and she would keep that promise.

Before she could say anything else, Bailey collapsed on the bed, balling up in pain. The pain was unlike anything she had ever experienced. But it was not as bad as she thought it would be. Then she looked up at Draven and realized that somehow he was shielding her from a lot of the pain. She was amazed at the power and strength that he possessed. When she looked into his eyes, she could see the pain that he was going through along with her. She loved him even more then.

She motioned for Draven to come closer, and as Draven bent down she whispered in his ear, "It's okay, I can take it. Just, please, hold me"

As soon as he let his guard down, the pain increased tenfold. He could see it on her face, but he understood that she had to do this on her own. So he did as she asked, holding her tight against his chest.

Draven could feel every bone in her body changing, and he kept telling himself that she would be free of pain when she finally shifted into her jaguar form. He could not stand to see her in pain.

Then it happened. He could feel the female jaguar getting closer to the surface, making her presence known. He quickly shifted into his jaguar form.

When he knew the last of her bones had altered to accommodate the jaguar, he grinned. "It is time, my love"

As a jaguar, her coat was cream-colored, soft and luxurious. He had never seen a Trigarian with a coat that color. To his amazement, her brilliant green eyes were not crystal blue, sharp and fierce. She was stunning, and she was all his.

Pressure was mounting on Lenex and his men. The time for an attack was nearing. Now more than ever, he felt the weight of his mission on his shoulders. They had to succeed. They just had to.

As night passed, they waited for the right time to strike them and take Alverez by surprise. Skyler shifted in to a jaguar and started the diversion. Now it was up to Lenex, Michael and the twins.

They could hear Skyler calling to the Pumarian males, taunting them and making his presence known. They could see the Pumarians' anxiety and rising anger as the jaguar challenged them. In a way, it was kind of amusing to the Trigarians who watched; they could smell an undercurrent of fear from their enemies.

Then it happened. Four of the six guards ran after Skyler to protect their land. In order for the plan to work, they needed to move fast. The twins split off to take care of the remaining guards.

They could see Alverez moving around in his study. The glass doors to the balcony hung open. They could smell the smoke from his Cuban cigar. They could hear the clinking of ice cubes in his drink.

Lenex and Michael were cautious as they shifted into their jaguar form. In that form, they easily scaled the wall to the study balcony. From there, Michael could see Alverez, standing with his back to them, poking at the fire to adjust one of the logs. Michael knew he could take off running, but it was a chance that they were going to have to take.

Slowly, as silently as he could, Michael crept over the balcony rail and slipped in through the open door. Lenex followed, tight on his heels.

He crouched, every muscle in his body tight. He shifted his weight on his back feet, readying for his pounce. Then with a loud snarl, he leapt straight for Alverez.

Mating with Bailey in jaguar form was the most beautiful thing that either one had experienced. The way that Bailey moved so fluidly and submitted to him it was incredible. Her snarling and the tension and power of her muscles invigorated him. When she reached her orgasm, her yowls reverberated off the walls, filling him with powerful desire.

Afterward, as they lay sweating and naked next to each other, Draven was surprised to feel Bailey's hand creeping down his belly. He'd thought she was asleep, but her brilliant green eyes were watching him from behind a curtain of red curls. She smiled at him as her fingers inched down to his groin.

Draven thought he was spent, but his body responded to her slow, seductive touch. Desire welled up in him again. He could smell her pheromones, heavy in the air. He jumped when she brushed his cock, and then groaned when she pulled away. He wanted her.

Bailey knew it. She loved teasing him. She stroked him slowly, feeling his dick grow hard under her fingers. She kissed his chest as he laid back, letting her win. For now.

She wanted to make him squirm. She wanted him to beg for release.

Bailey slid down his body, trailing her tongue from his neck to his nipple and down his stomach. She kissed teasingly around his navel. She knew what he wanted, but Bailey had her own ideas. Draven's head rolled back, his eyes closed.

Without warning, she swung her leg over his body, so that she sat in his lap, facing his feet. With a mischievous glance over her shoulder at Draven, she thrust him deep inside her and started rolling her hips. He couldn't hold his moans, it felt so good the way she tightened the muscles of her pussy around him.

Her hands twisted and danced above her head. He loved watching the way she moved on him – it was a fluid rolling that started at her hands, worked down through her arms and shoulders, and ended with her hips. Her long, red curls tumbled down her back, sweeping his chest. Her perky breasts jiggled and swayed with every movement. The muscles of her calves flexed tightly as she moved. When she leaned forward, her perky, finely curved ass just begged to be grabbed. She was amazing.

Bailey was grinding into him as hard as she could. Draven planted his hands on her hips, pushing himself deeper still.

She could feel his hips starting to buck

and thrust with her body, and knew he was approaching his finish. The heat was welling up inside her as his thrusting pushed her closer and closer to her orgasm. She began to pant as she gripped his thighs with her hands, increasing her speed.

Draven's hands were digging into her hips; it was almost painful how hard he was grabbing her. Still, she kept going. Faster. Harder.

Suddenly, he groaned and she felt his cock jerk within her as it released a stream of milky fluid. At the same time, wave after wave of pleasure rolled through her body.

She sat, panting, for a moment, with his dick still inside her. Draven's hands fell away from her hips. Now, he was spent. He sighed contentedly as she slid off him and curled up under his arm. Soon, her breathing slowed and deepened, and he knew she was fast asleep. He watched her sleeping, marveling at her beauty. And she was his, forever.

He thought again about her transformation. Still, he could not get passed the creamy white color of her coat. He wondered about it while she rested. Perhaps she was a hybrid of some sort? It didn't really matter to him what she was, but he would still have to look into it, that was for sure. For now, he wanted her to rest; later, he would show her what a true Trigarian did at night.

As he got up from the bed, he looked down at her and smiled; he knew she was the one for him and he was going to make sure that she enjoyed every minute of their life together. But first, he had to do some research to make sure that she was going to be okay.

Slipping on a pair of boxers, Draven went downstairs to the kitchen where the other men were waiting for him. "Is she alright?" Geoff asked.

Draven grinned back. "Yes, and it was well worth it, all of it." Pulling up a stool, he sat at the island looking at the two on the other side of the counter. "I have a question though - have either of you heard of a female Trigarian with a white or a cream-colored coat?"

"Why?" Darian asked, puzzled.

"When she shifts, Bailey's coat is creamy-white and her eyes are blue. I've never seen anything like it."

Darian looked at Draven. "Man, are you sure she was human?"

"Yes I am sure; I did not sense anything else, magical or otherwise. I just want to make sure that she is going to be okay. To my knowledge this has never happened to anyone in our race before."

Geoff was quiet, lost in thought, but Draven could tell that he was going to say something; it was written all over his face. "You could talk to the elders, see what they say. But you know how hard it is to get them to talk about history, especially when things like this happen."

Darian nodded.

"Then it is settled. Tomorrow at dawn we will set out to see the elders and get some answers." It was a long shot, but he was not willing to chance her life. She had given him everything in return for his love, and now it was his turn to give her all he had to keep her safe.

Just then, his phone rang. He snatched it up, eager for an update from the mission. It was Lenex.

"Alverez escaped, sir. He wasn't even here – it was a decoy. I'm sorry."

Draven hung up without saying a word.

6 A UNIQUE GIFT

God, she was so beautiful with the water careening off of her body. Draven felt so lucky to have Bailey by his side. He could stare at her body all day and never get tired of looking at it.

He had decided to bring her to his favorite spot, and now he watched her wash up from their late-night lovemaking. His men were a ways off; although her transformation was now complete, he didn't want the other males to become jealous. And, truthfully, he wasn't interested in hearing their smartass comments about how whipped he was. Granted he did not mind being whipped, she was incredible.

Draven knew that taking Bailey to see the elders could be dangerous, but he trusted his men to protect her. They would have to cross into some rough territory and he did not want her getting injured in any way during the trip. Draven would make sure she was watched carefully until she was comfortable using her new abilities.

As night slowly fell over them, Draven was still trying to figure out how to tell Bailey they had to leave town to go meet with the elders and she had to come with them. He didn't want to scare or anger her; he did not yet know the power she possessed. Draven also did not want her to think that something might be wrong with her.

After a while, he decided it would be best to let her believe it was sort of like a honeymoon. Trigarians did not really believe in marriage – only mating, which created a lifelong bond – but Bailey would not question him. It would be hard to explain why his team was coming, but he would deal with that later.

He was going to have to be careful to not slip up. Maybe he would have his men hang back a little so that Bailey would not notice them. But he would know they were there, and they would come quickly if they were needed.

When morning came, Draven and Bailey packed for a weeklong trip. He told her that he had a surprise for her: he was going to take her to his favorite place and have a romantic night with her. The best part was that it was on the way to see the elders.

Draven knew there was something different about her; even in human form, her senses were heightened. He hoped it was not anything serious, but it convinced him more than ever that he needed to seek the elders' advice.

As they finished the packing, Bailey was grinning from ear to ear. Draven did not think that he had ever seen her so happy. He wrapped his arms around her, kissing her neck and blowing in her ear. He could tell that she wanted him. He could smell the pheromones she gave off when he was nearby. But they had to start traveling soon; it was going to have to wait until later on. He kissed her one last time before he left the house to get the horses ready.

Bailey thought it was strange that Draven did not play with her when he was kissing her neck; usually he would take advantage of any opportunity to make love to her. Today, he seemed preoccupied. But with what? She would find out, one way or another.

Bailey was suddenly struck by an idea – one that always seemed to work.

She hurried into their stone shower room. It was perfect for making love – the walls hid the sound from anyone outside. She was known to get a little loud at times and he loved every minute of it.

When Draven came back to the mansion, Bailey was nowhere to be found. Where was she?

Then he heard the water running and knew she was in the shower. As hurried as he was, Draven had to admit he wanted her; apparently, she wanted him just as bad. He kicked off his shoes and started to strip on the way to the bathroom to join her.

Bailey looked amazing with the water running over her creamy soft skin. When she saw Draven, she gave him a mischievous grin.

"Oops... You found me."

She blew him a kiss and turned her body into the water. She knew exactly what she was doing to him. His cock was so hard he thought he was going to explode right there. Bailey began to run her hands all over her body, swaying to a slow rhythmical beat. She began to play with her breasts, squeezing them softly and running her hands down her tummy to her core, where she began to play with herself. She let out a soft moan.

That was it; he had to have her. He

stepped in the shower behind her, kissing her shoulders and neck, nibbling on her earlobe. She slowly turned to face him; she ran her hands over his chest and rubbed her body against his. He began to grind his cock against her. When they were moving together, Draven grabbed her by the hips and bent her over, pressing his cock into her core. He went slowly, sliding himself into her as she moaned.

Gently he pushed her body against the rock wall, running his hands over her body as he put his cock all the way into her and he began to make love to her. Her pussy felt incredible; he was groaning and panting and didn't care who heard him. Draven began to pump his cock into her, starting out slow and then speeding up and finally grinding his hips against her.

But he was not ready to finish yet. He took his cock out of her and began stroking it as she turned around to face him again. Bailey began kneeling down, smiling, ready to take his cock in her mouth. He stopped her, pulling her back up so she was standing in front of him.

"Not right now. I am here to take care of your needs. My needs can wait," he told her.

Kissing her passionately, he knew she had won – they would not be going anywhere anytime soon. He gave in. All he wanted at that moment was to pleasure every inch of her body.

With one quick movement, Draven shut off the water and carried her back to their bedroom. He laid her down on the bed and walked over to the door to close it. Draven would make love to her and make sure that she would be craving more later on. He loved when Bailey came to him in that babydoll he bought for her, begging him for a little attention and affection. He hoped that nighty would make an appearance or two during their trip.

She lay on the bed looking at him, as he climbed up on the bed between her legs. He knew that if he pushed the right buttons, he could get her to come right there. Instead, he was going to enjoy watching her squirm as he tenderly tortured her with his kisses and fingers.

Gently he kissed her inner thigh, running his hands over her hips to pull her black lace thong off. He admired her most secret beauty. He could tell that she was anxiously waiting for him to make love to her; she was already wet. He bent down and began blowing on her pussy while he played with it with his fingers. As he continued, he could hear her start to whine and moan quietly, trying not to be too loud. He wanted her to get louder.

"Come on, baby. Show me you love the things I do to you." Draven smirked knowing that she would give him what he wanted. Her cheeks were already turning red, and he knew that she was holding back. He wanted her to release the passion in her that she did know she possessed.

But Bailey was extremely strong-willed – more than he thought that she would be. When he noticed that she was able to hold it in, he knew that if he went down on her, she would come unglued and have an orgasm right there. Without saying a word, he positioned himself and began to flick her swollen pussy with the tip of his cock. It was not until then that her plan to play hard to get came undone.

The sweet assault made her come within seconds, but he was not done with her by any means. He was going to make sure that every inch of her was sated. Draven could feel her hands running over her body, softly pulling his hair as she continued to come. She was totally completely his. As her body arched in pleasure, it took all he had not to overpower her and take her as she lay right there in ecstasy and make her his over and over . But he wanted her to take control and do with him as she pleased. He was curious to see what she would do.

He rolled onto his back, pulling her on top of him. "Show me what you want from me. Don't hold back at all."

Grinning, Bailey began to ride his cock, moving her hips in a circular motion and running her hands over his chest, kissing his lips, neck, and chest. He could feel the animal in her wanting to be released. As she rode him, he whispered words of love to her. Arching his body, he pushed his cock deeper into her feminine core.

"Show me your power, love. Let the animal out. Don't hold back anything from me." The animal inside her heard his words, and she answered. Bailey tucked her hands under his shoulders, and as he drove his cock into her repeatedly, she dug her nails into him, arching her body. He felt incredible; she could not get enough of him. It was as if her body was going up in flames.

Without warning, she climbed off of him and positioned herself in front of him on her hands and knees, presenting her backside to him. He knew what she wanted, but he was going to tease her a little first. While on his knees behind her, Draven inserted just the tip of his cock into her and pulled it out. He did this for a few minutes until Bailey emitted a low, purring growl.

With that, he picked up the pace, taking her from behind. God, she felt incredible as he drove his cock into her repeatedly. It took all he had not to start pumping harder and harder until she screamed in submission.

Then he had a thought – why not take her to the oasis for the night and make love to her there? There, they could change into the jaguar form and the animal inside of her wouldn't have to hold back. He could feel the animal in her begging for release, and he wanted to give it to her.

But first, he would satiate her. After that, he would take her to the oasis and make love to her again. And they would be moving closer to the elders and, hopefully, some answers about Bailey's strange transformation. Was it a gift or a curse? Only time and the elders would be able to say.

For now, he would bring her pleasure as she had never experienced it before. As he inserted his cock into her and began rocking his hips back and forth, Bailey matched his pace. She wrapped her arm around his neck as he sped up, his pace driving his cock harder and faster into her. He ran his hands all over her body, playing with her perky breasts, pulling at them lightly. As he did, she responded with a moan and her hips ground against him in a circular motion. She moaned louder as she began to play with herself as he continued to pound into her.

"Oh yes, baby.... Just like that. Mmm.... Harder. Make me come again." Draven had counted at least four orgasms, and he was not done with her yet. As she continued to moan, she took the fingers from her pussy and put them in his mouth. She tasted incredible, so sweet. He had to have more of her.

Perhaps they would not make it to the oasis by nightfall after all.

7 ALL TIED UP

After two and a half hours of fiery sex, Bailey's ravenous sexual appetite finally subsided, and she slowly drifted off to sleep. Draven knew that it would not be long before she woke and wanted more. He was getting a little worn out from all of their late-night trysts, but he certainly wouldn't deny her another. He'd heard from the other males that during the first few months after a female's transformation, she would have a voracious sex drive. It would eventually pass; until it did, it was his job to satisfy her every need.

He thought again about the oasis and taking her there to teach her the ways of the Trigarians. But before he could get up and get his wits about him, he fell fast asleep with his arms wrapped around Bailey.

When Draven woke up the next morning, he was surprised to find Bailey on her knees, just about to get on top of him and begin to ride him again.

"You know, you were not supposed to wake up yet," she giggled. "I was going to give you a good morning surprise. I mean, how can I resist when you're stiff as a board and so incredibly tempting?"

She looked like an animal ready to pounce on her prey. God, she looked amazing. Grinning, he pulled her on top of him, sliding his cock into her. She was so tight and slick. He knew they needed to get going, but what was he supposed to do? Between his throbbing hard-on and this beautiful naked woman crawling over him, Draven was nearly ready to explode as he slid into her tight, hot core. He had to have her, just one last time before they left.

Bailey was arching back and riding his cock. As she rode him, he could feel her pick up her pace. She was getting close to having an orgasm and it felt so good. The closer she got, the tighter she became and the closer he was to having an orgasm himself.

Bailey emitted a low, throaty jaguar yowl. The female in her wanted to be released, but Draven was still worried that she would be hurt. Bailey hadn't learned to control the animal within her yet.

He slowed Bailey down, trying to calm her fervor, but it did not work. She was so frantic while riding him that he had to lift her off and take control of the situation.

Draven pinned her to the bed, spread her legs, and started to go down on her, assaulting her pussy with his mouth. He could not believe that she tasted so good. Strangely, it tasted sweeter than it had before her transformation.

"Mmm.... Baby, come for me. That's it. Right there."

As she came in his mouth, she arched her body and writhed on the bed. But he was not done with her by any means; he was just getting started. Draven could not believe that he wanted her again; it was as if she started a chain reaction between the two of them. He didn't understand it. He only knew that it felt extraordinary.

As Draven looked down at Bailey, the evidence of their lovemaking was on her face. She was flushed and her heart was racing. But he could tell that she was ready for him again. Damn, she was good and she could keep up.

He grinned. "You and I are going to keep each other very busy, aren't we?"

Smiling, she looked up at him. "Are you complaining that I can't keep my hands off you?"

"Not at all," he said, kissing her neck and massaging her ample breasts. He pulled at her nipples lightly and then let his hands wander all over her body. She was a goddess to him. She was everything he ever wanted in a mate and more. He kissed her stomach and began blowing on her hips, working his way down. Bailey closed her eyes, enjoying the sweet torture that she was receiving.

"How could this get any better?" she thought. It was the best sex that she had ever had, and she would not trade it for anything. Draven looked up at her and started to chuckle.

"You do remember that I can read your thoughts, right?"

She laughed. "Sorry, I'm not used to that."

He sat up and looked at her with mischievous eyes. "But there are a few things that we could do that I think you would love. Just lay there for a minute. I'll be right back."

Grinning, she did what he asked, waiting impatiently until he returned. When he came back, Draven had what looked like a feather and a few lengths of rope. She was curious and excited to find out what he had planned.

"Now do me a favor and lay in the middle of the bed for a moment. We can do this in two ways: both your feet are tied down and you cannot move your legs, or we bind your wrists and your arms. Your choice."

She positioned herself on the bed so that he was able to tie her arms to the bed. She would not be able to move unless he allowed it. Once he felt she was secure enough, he pulled out some rose oil, put a little on his hands, and rubbed it into her flesh. Then he took what looked like a feather and positioned himself between her legs, blowing on her core and using the feather to caress the sensitive skin. It took everything that she had to control herself. She wanted to come unglued right then, but she would not give in just yet.

"How does that feel, baby?" He could see that she was holding back and that it would take a little more to push her over the edge. She was going to play hard to get.

He adjusted the ropes so that she was rested on her knees, with her arms above her head. He grabbed a hold of her ass and began to dart his tongue in and out of her pussy. At first she kind of jumped when his tongue touched her swollen pussy. The more he did it, the more she reacted; soon, she was grinding on him as he continued. She began to moan; the louder she moaned, the more it excited him. He would have to have her soon, or he would pass out from the throbbing pressure in his cock. By now he was so hard it was actually almost painful; he was going to have to get relief soon, or else.

With a loud, long moan, she came in his mouth. He untied her and laid her on their bed, lying next to her as he brushed her nipples with his fingertips. Her nipples were nice and perky. He loved that her body responded to his touch every single time.

"I love you, Bailey Marie."

She smiled at him. "I love you, too, Draven."

She glanced down at Draven's hardened cock. "Oh my! Are you just happy to see me, or are you like this all the time?" She laughed.

Droplets of precum glistened on the head of his cock. He wanted to be in her so bad. She reached down and wiped the precum off with her finger, then licked the finger clean. "Mmmm." She looked up into his eyes.

Bailey was playing with fire, and she knew it. That one action turned him on even more; he was about ready to pounce on her and just let her have it. It was what she was waiting for. She loved it when he was aggressive with her.

Before she knew it, Draven had picked her up and set her down in his lap, then on his cock. He began to pound her pussy as fast as he could. God, he was so good.

She came three more times before he was done with her. When he was finally done, he kissed her deeply while softly touching her face. "You are truly amazing, Bailey. You are the only one I want."

He gently laid her back on the bed and began to get dressed. When he looked back at Bailey, she was sleeping. He wondered if the elders would be able to tell him anything about Bailey's unique transformation and what kind of power she might possess. It worried him that there was something wrong with her and he did not know what it was or if there was anything that they could do for her. He only hoped that he had not condemned her to her death.

Being a female Trigarian was risky enough as it was. Many females suffered complications during the birthing process. Often, the child survived, but the female did not. It was just one of the trials that Trigarians faced when they found their mate. And since they mated for life, losing one's mate meant a lifetime of loneliness. If something happened to Bailey, no one could take her place. Males would wander for years, searching for peace and wholeness. There would be a hole in their hearts that could never be filled again. Many killed themselves rather than live that way.

Draven now understood why the males of his species were so protective of their females. He gave them a great deal of respect as well. He knew that eventually Bailey would have to know all of the things that he did; she would have to be able to protect herself. It wouldn't be like it was before, where she did not have to worry when she went to town. Now, she was one of them. She had to make sure that she could protect not only herself but also their children when the time came.

Draven grinned looking down at Bailey. Children. Wow, that was not something he had thought of before. He smiled at the thought of Bailey one day being the mother of his children. Man, would those kids be a handful. He chuckled a little. If they were half as stubborn and bullheaded as he and Bailey could be, they were in trouble. He would have to watch them carefully when they were older. But he was up for the challenge. He was still getting used to the idea that Bailey was so calm about becoming one of his kind. It made him happy that she chose to be with him.

He nuzzled his face against her long, flowing, curly hair. She was his fiery little sex kitten.

He loved how her hair always smelled of jasmine and lavender and how her bright green eyes shimmered when she looked into his. Draven could see how much she loved him in her eyes and the way her body moved. She was truly a godsend. Now, it was his turn to make sure that she was safe. But he was not going to wake her right now. He was enjoying being able to hold her and play with her hair as he watched her sleep.

Draven was amazed at how peaceful she was when she was sleeping. But he had to admit that when he was next to her, all he could think about was making love to her this morning and tasting the sweet juices of her womanly core as she came in his mouth.

It was too bad that they needed to leave before too long. He knew that he was going to have to wait until they got to the oasis before he made love to her again. They had to get to the elders soon. Something just felt a little off this morning. Something was not quite right with Bailey. But what was it?

He slid out of bed, put his velour robe on, and left, heading to the study.

In the study, he sat in his antique high backed chair. All he could think about was getting Bailey to the elders to make sure she was okay. His men had returned, empty-handed. That Alverez was still on the loose and that they had no idea where he might be only made the situation more precarious.

8 YOUR SECRET IS SAFE WITH ME

When Bailey woke up, Draven was gone. For a moment, she feared he had left on another mission. She wanted him home with her. But no, he wouldn't leave without telling her.

She felt different than she had yesterday. There was something new, but what was it? Should she tell Draven? What was there to say?

All she could think of was the way she felt when Draven had tied her up that morning – the sweet ecstasy that she felt as he went down on her, holding her still in his arms as she continued to grind on his face. Damn, he was good. She wanted more of him.

Looking around the room to ensure she really was alone, Bailey slid one hand down her smooth belly and began to gently caress the outside of her slit. Imagining Draven was watching her, she felt her juices start to flow. Carefully, she inched her forefinger inwards, slowly opening her slit. Her finger found her magic button and moved in circles around it. Her body was flush with heat and she began to breathe heavier. Bailey closed her eyes and imagined Draven sitting across the room, secretly watching her enjoy this private time.

She imagined Draven feeling the pressure building against his pants and then pulling out his cock. She increased her pace as she imagined Draven slowly stroking his rod, a look of pleasure and lust on his face. Overcome with voyeuristic yearning, Draven began to stroke faster and faster, thoroughly enjoying watching Bailey pleasure herself. Soon, Bailey couldn't stand it anymore. She imagined Draven groaning loudly as long streams spurted from his cock. She came at the same time, arching her back and riding the waves of ecstasy.

As her breathing slowed, she opened her eyes and stared across the room at the empty space where she imagined he sat. Bailey smiled, wishing she could stay in bed forever, pleasuring herself. But right now she was going to go take a shower and cleanse herself of the early morning session of lovemaking with Draven as well as the imagined one. Then she was going to put on some lounging clothes, something loose and not so revealing; she did not feel too confined in her clothes.

In the shower, Bailey let the water wash over her body. She closed her eyes and leaned against the shower wall. All of a sudden, she felt as if there was an added weight on her and she needed to brace herself. The feel of the water on her body was incredible; she did not realize that Draven was standing at the shower door, watching her and admiring her body.

God, she looked beautiful with the water careening off of her body. Her nipples were perky, her skin pale and slick. He could stare at her body all day and never get tired of looking at her. It was not until he was in the shower with her that she opened her eyes, jumping because she had not even heard him enter the bathroom.

Smiling up at him, she wondered if he could see that something was on her mind. As she looked into his eyes, she could almost swear that she saw the beast that was inside him calling to her, begging for release. She didn't have the strength to do anything this morning. She wished that she could reach out to the animal within him and borrow his strength to finish her shower.

Although she knew the thought of it was silly, she had heard of some individuals who could speak to other people telepathically. It was a long shot, and she knew it. She thought she would try it and see if the beast inside of Draven would hear her. Draven laughed, holding her, keeping her balanced and unable to fall.

"You know I am not a beast, and yes, I can hear your thoughts. I just haven't talked to you this way yet. I thought you'd want some privacy."

She blushed. She kept forgetting he could hear her thoughts. Looking into Bailey's eyes, Draven could see not only the embarrassment but also the hurt she felt for calling him a beast. Then he heard her next thought and broke into a wide grin.

Without a word, he leaned in against her, locking his lips to hers. She melted into him, her hands running across his finely muscled chest.

Draven took a bar of soap and began lathering up his hands. He ran his hands up her arms, leaving thick, soft foam over her skin. He rubbed down her shoulders and gently lathered her chest, carefully circling her nipples. Then he rubbed down her stomach and the soft triangle of hair below her navel. Bailey let the hot water stream down her body, washing the suds away.

He turned her around so she was facing the wall. Bailey leaned against it, loving the feel of the smooth tile against her skin. His hand worked a thick lather over her body, starting at her neck and shoulders. He worked in small circles down her back, working her tired muscles. Then he crossed down to her buttocks and lingered there, covering her hips and ass with white suds.

She felt his cock, thick and hard, sliding against her skin. She pushed back slightly, encouraging him to rub harder against her. Now, he was sliding his cock between her butt cheeks. The soap made everything slick and much more sensitive. Bailey was tired, but it felt so good.

Draven's hands were on her hips as he ground his pelvis into her. She could feel his body tensing as his pace increased. He was getting close. She pushed back harder, moaning.

With a groan, he pushed against her one last time, shooting his thick white stream on her back and ass. It quickly dissolved away in the hot water.

The steam from the shower was suddenly stifling. A wave of dizziness overtook Bailey. As she swayed, he reached out to stabilize her. "Are you alright?"

She looked down, unsure if she should say anything, but then it just came out of nowhere. "Draven, I think there is something wrong with me. I woke up this morning not feeling like myself, if you know what I mean. It is like there is this extra weight. I feel...off balance."

Draven took a minute and turned her around so that her back was in front of him, wrapping his arms around her to keep her from falling.

It was then that he knew that he was going to have to get her to the elders fast. He could see there was something seriously wrong with her. After washing up he helped her to the bedroom, where she sat on the edge of the bed and tried to stand, only to fall back onto the bed.

What was going on?

He helped her with her clothes and then carried her down the stairs to the brown leather loveseat that was in her den. From there, he proceeded to look her over. There was nothing wrong with her that he could see, but that did not mean that there was not something else that they were not seeing.

After looking her over, he was more puzzled than anything. "Honey, close your eyes and rest. I am going to call someone and see if they can go with us on a trip to see the elders. That way my full attention is on you the whole time."

She looked into his eyes, gave him a faint grin, and closed her eyes. Usually she would fight him, insisting that she was alright; she did neither of those things. It was time to get the men together and make their way to the elders before it was too late.

His men were still patrolling the house, but it would take a while to get the supplies ready for the trip. He gave the orders, and they scrambled to make preparations. It would take a day and a half to reach the elders. Draven knew they had to leave today, even given the late hour. Come hell or high water, he was going to get her to the elders.

All that they had to do now was to get Bailey there safely and hope that none of Alverez's men tried anything while they were traveling.

Still, Draven was worried that if someone did attack them, Bailey would be completely helpless. It was in her best interests to get at least a crash course on her new abilities, even if it only aided a hasty escape. They could teach her to run faster and hide much easier from those who were hunting her. They all hoped it would not come to that. It would take a lot of concentration, strength, and willpower for her to stay in Trigarian form.

When the men were ready to leave, they went out to their horses while Draven woke Bailey. She was still a little off balance, but not as bad as she was before. He smiled at her. "Why don't you and I ride together? That way we can make sure you make it there in one piece."

He chuckled, trying to make light of the situation. He wanted to be able to easily monitor her health and keep her protected until they reached the next town. They walked out to the stables to get his horse, Zeus, and Draven noticed that she was a little skittish around the stallion. Taking her by the hand, he led Bailey to Zeus' side and began to pet the horse on the nose.

"Like this, love. See? He won't hurt you." Her hands were trembling as she petted the horse. When she was not looking, Draven whispered in her ear and rubbed her lower back. To her amazement, she became more attuned to her surroundings and the horse standing in front of her. He was beautiful, and she was not so afraid of him anymore. With that, Draven kissed her neck.

"Do you trust me?" he asked, as he mounted Zeus.

She stumbled back a little bit as the horse pranced forward and then back again. Once he knew that Zeus was stable, he reached for Bailey's arm and pulled her up in front of him, making sure that she was secure as they took off from the stables. He rode out to the front of the mansion where his men were waiting for them. Draven reiterated the plan, and they began to ride. They all knew that Bailey was to be guarded at all costs until the elders told them what it was exactly that Bailey had inside of her.

They decided to set up camp for the night in Themeon Forest. It was a lush and beautiful forest. Darian and Skyler would patrol the area; Draven and Bailey would rest so they could start fresh in the morning.

While they rode, Bailey's exhaustion had overcome her. With Draven arms around her, she dreamt.

In her dream, she swam naked in a deep, clear pool in the middle of a dense jungle. She could hear the calls of the birds echoing through the air. Everywhere she looked was green. The jungle seemed to call out to her, asking her to run through its trees and climb through its branches.

Draven floated on his back near her, also naked. He didn't speak: neither of them did. But they smiled at each other as they came together. Their limbs intertwined, they were floating together. He kissed her, drawing her in close to him. She gave in to his strength, floating along as his lips grazed her skin.

His hands were on her breasts and she could feel his manhood swelling against her leg. The water seemed to support them – they didn't need to kick or swim. His finger found her clit, tracing small circles against it. She moaned, rolling her head back in the water. Her hair spread out like a curtain behind her, floating red gold against the deep blue.

Then his fingers were sliding inside her, prying, searching, digging deeper. She wrapped her legs around his waist, her breasts bobbing in the water before him. As she kissed him, she pushed herself down, thrusting his cock inside her. Now his head rolled back as he sank a little deeper in the water. He was thrusting up into her, driving his cock as deep as he could. She was wrapped around him, kissing his neck, nibbling his ears.

It felt amazing, unlike anything she had felt before. Even the slightest touch set off fireworks, ripples of pleasure that traveled through her whole body. As he ground harder into her, the ripples became waves, each more powerful than the last.

"Harder," she was whispering, begging him to take her. "Harder, baby."

Suddenly his hands were on her shoulders, shaking her gently. Bailey's eyes snapped open to find Draven staring down at her. There was a mixture of concern and amusement in his eyes. He grinned. "Good dream?"

She blushed and did not say a word.

As Draven lowered her off of Zeus, he whispered, "Don't worry. Your secret is safe with me." Grinning, he noticed that she looked a little better than she did at the mansion, and he was glad. Maybe all she needed was some rest and a change of scenery.

When they had finished setting up camp, Draven took Bailey by the hand and led her to a place that very few people knew of – an oasis that had a white sand beach and a waterfall. It was a beautiful sight to see. "It is almost as beautiful as you," Draven told her.

She blushed, "Thank you." As they walked down to the beach, she looked around the area and noticed a little hut over by the waterfall. Was there anyone in there?

"You don't have to worry. This is my spot, where I go to get away from all of the chaos once in a while. When I need a break." Bailey relaxed, smiling at him. She wrapped her arms around him and kissed him passionately.

"Thank you," she whispered.

Puzzled, he looked into her eyes. "For

what, honey?"

"For making me part of your life, your world, all that you do. You've shown me that not all guys are just out for one thing after all. You really are my knight in shining armor, and that means a lot to me."

Draven could see that she meant every word that she said. Tears were welling up in her eyes as she looked at him. Scooping her up in his arms, he carried her to the hut. Inside the hut she felt a sense of peace; all of the tension seemed to leave her body. She was astounded at how big the hut was when she was inside it. It was bigger than it looked.

"Looks can be deceiving," Bailey said, and Draven chuckled.

"Yes, they most certainly can. That's kind of why I brought you down here." She was suddenly kind of worried about why she was there. Was there something wrong with her?

"No, there is nothing wrong with you. I want to show you some things that you may need to know if you need to protect yourself."

She let out a sigh of relief. "But I already know how to protect myself. I took self-defense classes in college."

He put his hands on her shoulders. "Honey, while it's great that you can handle yourself against humans, you may come across some individuals who are, shall we say, non-human. Like Alverez and his men."

Bailey remembered her one encounter with some of Alverez's men; she did not want a repeat of that night.

"The reason I brought you down here was so that we would have a little more privacy while I am teaching you, and so no one would bother us." Kissing her on the forehead, he backed away. "Now what I am going to do is teach you the way of the Trigarians. I promise I will not harm you in any way. What I want to do is to show you how to defend yourself. Then you do yourself. Do you understand?"

She shook her head yes, still adjusting to the fact that she was now part animal.

Draven shifted into his jaguar form and then watched Bailey as she shifted. They ran out the front of the hut. He still could not believe how beautiful she was with her cream-colored coat and dazzling crystal blue eyes. As he circled her, he noticed that she seemed bigger when she shifted. He thought maybe it was because she had not been working out lately.

As he taught her the different ways to protect and defend herself, he was amazed at how fast she was picking things up. It was like she was a sponge; if he showed her something once, she had it down to a science.

When they were done, he ran under the waterfall. She was not far behind. When they were behind the waterfall, Draven changed back into his human form. The cool spray on his skin felt so good.

Damn, he was sexy after working with her. She wanted him so bad she could taste his kisses on her lips. Carefully, she changed back into human form and stood under the fall, letting the water run over her body.

To Draven, every single inch of her skin was beautiful. He was glad that he had decided to bring her to his favorite spot, but he wasn't in any way done with her. He would claim her again tonight in animal form for the first time since the transformation, and he would make sure that she loved every minute of it.

Carefully, he came up behind her and began to massage her breasts slowly, blowing in her ear and rubbing his cock against her. He just wanted to feel her body against his at first. But when he heard a soft moan, his cock seemed to jump and come to attention right away. It was right then that he knew he had to have her now. As he played with her breasts, she began to grind up against his cock. Then she started to reach around to his cock, sliding her hand up and down his shaft, squeezing just enough to make his cock swell a little more.

Damn, he may not be able to wait until tonight. The beast inside of him wanted her now, to be inside of her and claim her as his mate. He lifted her up, wrapping her legs around his waist, and began to make love to her. He wanted to make sure that she was loosened up for his cock before he shifted into the jaguar. She felt so good he almost did not want to stop.

Setting her down, he shifted and waited for her to shift as well. It took her a minute, but she figured it out. Then they would mate and run without confines, free in the wild.

9 SURPRISES REVEALED

After making love to Bailey in jaguar form, Draven felt as if there was more of a connection between them than ever before. He was lying next to her while she slept on a pad that he had made for them. He turned the gas lanterns on and looked around; he was going to have to carry her back to camp or let the men know where they were so they would not worry.

Bailey looked like an angel wrapped up in the red satin sheets. Her face was still a little flushed and her breasts were perky from the cool air in the hut. He could not believe how beautiful she was, and she was his forever. He ran his hands through her curly, red hair, caressing her face and running his thumb over her lips. Her skin was so soft and welcoming. Draven could not help himself; he had to kiss them.

Finally, he pulled himself away from her. He was only going to let his men know that they were somewhere close and they would be back by dawn. She would be fine for a short while.

He shifted into his jaguar form and ran out of the hut. When he reached the campsite, Lenex, Michael, Landon, and Geoff were sitting around a fire talking quietly amongst themselves, careful not to be too loud. Darian, Skyler, and Ty were patrolling the area.

He was glad to see that his men took their job so seriously. Draven was anxious; Alverez's men had not shown their faces since they tried to take Bailey from him. And they had no idea where Alverez himself could be. Draven was going to be guarding Bailey until they found out what made her different from the other females.

A bloodcurdling scream broke through the night. It was Bailey.

Draven bolted for the hut; his men were tight on his heels. Draven could hear her heavy breathing; he could smell her fear in the air. She was threatened, and Draven knew it.

When Draven and his men arrived, they found four of Alverez's men surrounding Bailey as if she was a spectacle to be watched. They crouched around her, pacing back and forth, hissing and snarling at her.

Draven leapt into the air with a fierce growl. Then he saw what they saw – Bailey had shifted into her jaguar form, but instead of sparkling blue, her eyes were blood red.

The Pumarians surrounded her, preventing her from fleeing, but they would not approach her. It was as if they were afraid to even touch her. She was hissing and growling at them as fiercely as any Trigarian female would. She fought with the ferocity of a mother protecting her cubs.

Draven paused at that thought. Cubs. Pregnant. Could that be why she has been feeling so off during the last couple of days?

He didn't have much time to consider it. Bailey looked like she was about to kill the intruders. But she was new to this form, and the Pumarians were strong. There was too much risk that she would be injured. She was doing exactly what he'd taught her to protect herself, but now it was his turn.

Before he crashed into Alverez's men, Draven had one last thought – if Bailey was pregnant, he would not have to worry about the other males. Once a female is with a child, she is considered to be no good to other males. Still, he knew that he had to protect her even more now.

Then, he noticed another male lurking in the shadows near the entrance to the hut. Larger, sulking, and aggressive. Draven recognized his scent at once.

Bastian Alverez.

Pouncing on one of the larger males, Draven attacked. He and his men quickly engaged the Pumarians. Bailey danced around, frightened and angry, as the fighting raged around her. With Lenex at his side, Draven cut a path through to Bailey. But he was torn – protect Bailey or engage Alverez.

The Pumarian leader had thrown himself into the fight, unable to resist the rising aggression inside him. He threw his weight against Landon, moving in to clamp down on the Trigarian's neck. Death by strangulation was the Pumarian way.

Lenex was at Draven's side the whole time. With an angry chuff, he gestured his second-in-command toward Alverez. Without hesitation, Lenex leapt for his target. Their earlier failure to capture Alverez still stung; he was eager to make up for it.

In the end, Alverez's men were outnumbered and they fell quickly. With a sharp snap, Geoff dispatched the last of the men. Together, Lenex and Landon cornered Alverez; Landon pinned him down while Lenex clamped down on his throat, suffocating him. Draven watched tensely, feeling great relief when Alverez gasped his last breath.

"I thought you said that they were not going to come after me again, Draven. You lied to me," her voice screamed in his head. Bailey looked at him with tears in her eyes; he could see pain and sadness there.

When the Pumarians were beaten, Draven shifted back to his human form and instructed the men to keep a sharp eye out for more of Alverez's men. With their boss now dead, they could seek revenge. And if they found out that Bailey was pregnant, they would kill her without hesitation just to get back at Draven. Surely they would quickly figure out that he and his team were headed for the elders.

Draven moved toward Bailey as she shifted back into her human form. He kneeled down next to her and held her for a short time. He brushed her hair away from her tear-stained face. Whispering in her ear, he said, "Honey, I really did not know that they were close to us. I thought no one knew about this place except me. I thought you'd be safe. I am so sorry that this happened to you. From now on, I will not leave your side. I swear it." She gave him a small smile and kissed his cheek.

Draven nuzzled the side of her face and ran his hands through her hair. "I will never put you or our child in any danger as long as I live." Bailey chuckled.

"Child? What child?"

Draven looked at her, scrambling to cover his tracks. "Well, you know what I mean. I would protect you and our children when the time came. Until then, you are safe with me."

Draven didn't want to tell her right now that he suspected that she was with a child. He thought he might talk to the men; see if they had noticed anything, before he talked to her. He didn't want to cause her unneeded stress.

By afternoon, they would be with the elders; Draven hoped they would be able to provide him some answers about Bailey. But for now, he was going to try to help her to relax. He would take her back to the waterfall and give her a full body massage.

Pulling Bailey to her feet, he led her down to the water. A little hesitant at first, she was reluctant to move out into the open at first. Eventually, she relented. Draven striped her down and led her into the water. She looked amazing underneath the moonlight in the water.

As they stood together under the waterfall, he held her close to him. He could still feel the tension in her body, her heart still racing.

"It will be alright love. I promise. We will get through this and then we will go somewhere to escape for a while. No missions, I promise. Just you and I."

She laughed at him, kissing his cheek. "I know you. You wouldn't be able to stay away from your men if they had to go on a mission. You would be right there with them. It's your duty to keep them safe and out of harm's way. I wouldn't expect anything less from you. It's who you are. It's who you will always be."

Holding on to him tightly, Bailey listened to his heartbeat. It was strong and solid, and she found hers slowing down to match its rhythm. She would be safe on this trip, and she knew it. But she did think it was nice to get away from Draven's men, just for a little while.

"I will hold you to that promise, though. You and me, escaping for a while. No missions to worry about." With that she pushed her body up against his and began to blow in his ear. She could feel his body starting to respond to her touch. Perhaps it was the rush of adrenaline from the attack, but suddenly she just had to have him.

Bailey began to run her hands all over his body, kissing his chest and his abs. He was built like a Greek god. And he was all hers.

She grinned, looking up into his beautiful green eyes. "I love you, Draven. More than life itself. I will always love you no matter what. No matter how old we get, I will always be by your side." But even after she said those words to him, Draven still wasn't relaxing. His eyes were scanning her body, checking for even the most minor of injuries. She sighed. "I am fine, love."

Brushing his face with her hand, Bailey led him back behind the waterfall and pushed him against the rock wall. She was going to make love to him like never before.

She began running her hands all over his tanned, muscular body, kissing his neck and working her way down to his chest and abs while her hand went down to his already hard shaft .

'Mmm... I think someone is excited to see me,' she thought, sliding her hand up and down his already erect cock. She knew he was ready to go when she felt the precum on the tip of his cock. Seeing that glistening fluid made her even more excited.

She got down on her knees in the water and began to suck on his cock, licking the tip of his cock clean and then licking her lips before she continued to suck on him. She could hear him moaning louder and louder, wanting more. She enjoyed having this power over him; at any moment she could bring him to his knees. She loved to watch his expressions as she sucked on his cock. She knew what he wanted: he was tempted to drive his cock further into her mouth. His hips were rotating and thrusting gently as he moaned. She took her time and teased him a little more before she put his entire cock in her mouth.

He went completely still and Bailey thought he was going to lose it right there. Instead, he picked her up and pinned her against the wall, thrusting his cock into her warm pussy. She had succeeded. He was hungry for her as she was for him, and that was exactly the way she liked it. The sweet assault that he was now giving her was exactly what she had been hoping for.

"Oh, yes. Baby, yes. Give that cock to me."

She held on to his neck as he continued to pound his cock into her. Her breasts bounced higher as he thrust his shaft into her.

After so many years of feeling like a

beast because of the animal inside of him, now he had someone who did not see the beast as a threat. Bailey saw him, and that was all that he wanted from anyone. He needed to be seen as a human, not as an animal. But just then, it was the animal in control.

He could feel her getting closer and closer to climaxing, but he did not want her to quit yet. He had plans for her.

Draven carried her out of the waterfall and deeper into the cave. There was another larger room that could not be seen from the waterfall entrance. The walls sparkled with diamond and gold fragments. Boxes of emergency supplies and rations were stacked around the room. Bailey had to give him credit – Draven was prepared for anything, it seemed.

Then she saw the bed.

It was a four-post oak bed covered by a blue comforter and light blue satin sheets. It was beautiful. Draven laid her down in the middle of the bed. She could tell that he was up to trouble just by the way he was acting; she was enjoying every little minute of it.

Draven came back with a smirk on his face. Crawling up between her legs, he began kissing her thighs and licking her pussy, darting his tongue in and out. Then he began to massage her hips while looking up at her. She looked beautiful as she arched her body to meet his mouth. He could tell that her body was about to go up in flames if he did not calm the fire that was burning inside of her.

She wanted him now.

10 GYPSY'S GIFT

Before Draven could do anything more, Bailey flipped him on his back and began to ride him. He was shocked at the strength she possessed. He did not say a word; he just enjoyed every moment as she rode his cock, driving it deeper into her. As she rode him, she placed his hands on her breasts so that he could play with them. He loved to suckle on them as she rode on his cock. He began to pull gently on her breasts, pinching her nipples between his fingers.

God, her breasts were amazing. He loved the fullness and weight of them in his hands. As he flicked her nipples with his tongue and massaged her breasts, Bailey emitted a soft moan that became a deep growl.

Grinning, he picked Bailey up off of his cock and repositioned her in front of him, putting her on her hands and knees. He came up behind her and put his head between her legs so that her pussy was just a few inches from his mouth.

As he tasted her sweet juices, she lifted herself up so that she was on her just knees and she was able to grind her pussy on his tongue. He let her stay like that for a moment, but eventually he pulled her back down on all fours.

"Now, come for me, love. Give it to me." He watched her face as she came in his mouth. Her cheeks were flushed and her body was warm, but he could tell that she had yet to be sated.

Sliding out from underneath her, he repositioned himself behind her and gently pushed his cock into her core. God, she was so tight. He began to rock back and forth, sliding his cock in and out of her. She shifted and moaned, pressing back against him. He ran his hands down her arms and then back up to cup her breasts. As her moaning intensified, he started massaging her breasts, feeling their weight and softness in his palms. He twisted the nipples, sending shivers down her back.

Bailey pushed back hard against him, begging for more. He increased the speed and ferocity of his thrusts, grinding his pelvis into her. With each thrust he dove deeper. Her muscles clenched around his cock. Her fingers were digging into the mattress as she braced herself against him. Her breasts bounced and jiggled in his hands.

Sweat trickled down his face. It dripped from his nose and jaw onto her glistening back. He didn't notice. His eyes were closed as he grunted and groaned. Her cries and moans rose up to meet his. Together, their volume and pace increased until finally he couldn't take it anymore. With a loud grunt, Draven pushed his cock as deep into her as he could and released his load. Bailey cried out from her own orgasm, all the muscles in her body trembling.

As she collapsed to the bed on her belly, panting, Draven laid down next to her, sated. He began to massage her back. The tension began to melt away as his fingers kneaded her flesh. Soon, she was fast asleep. He curled up behind her, holding her tight, never wanting to let go of her.

As soon as dawn approached, Bailey and the men were back on the road to the elders. Draven looked down at Bailey; he could see that she was still tired. He tried to shift a little so she would be more comfortable, leaning into the hollow of his body. If she was carrying their child, even riding a short distance could be uncomfortable and potentially risky for the child's health. Until he knew for sure whether she was with a child, he had to prioritize her health.

His men had seen no trace of any more of Alverez's men overnight. As they rode, he kept his head up, scenting the air. With Alverez dead, he hoped the Pumarians would back off.

Still, he could not wait to get to the elders and get some answers.

Only a few hours later, they had reached a mansion with giant trees and foliage so overgrown the garden looked like a jungle. Draven could feel peace coming over all of the men. It was as if they could take a minute and just relax; they had reached their destination. As they rode up to the gated mansion, Draven noticed someone watching from one of the windows. He recognized one of the elders at once.

As the men and Bailey approached the door, they were greeted by the butler, Goddrick. He took them into the sitting room and left them waiting for the elder Kelden.

Kelden was an older gentleman, tall, with long, white flowing hair and the brightest blue eyes. He greeted the men and Bailey, kissing Bailey's hand as a sign of respect. Kelden sat behind the desk, Draven sat near enough to speak to him comfortably, while Lenex and the others took up positions on the outskirts of the room. When Draven told him that Bailey shifted into a cream-colored jaguar, Kelden looked back at her, raising an eyebrow and smiling at her.

When they were finished, Kelden asked the men to wait in the study while he and Draven took care of Bailey. As they left, there was a moment of silence.

As the doors closed behind them, Kelden turned to Bailey. "Child, what do you know of your family's history?"

Bailey thought about it for a moment. "Not much. Both of my parents were killed when I was young. When I was at the orphanage, I was passed around to three different families until I was old enough to be on my own. I try not to think about the orphanage much."

"Do you remember anything about your parents? A last name? Something that they gave you or told you?" Draven asked her.

Bailey stared down at the floor. "Nothing that really makes sense. But they did give me this," she offered, pulling out a coin with a gypsy crest on one side and a cat on the other. Curious as to what it meant, he handed it to Kelden.

After studying it for a while, Kelden looked back at Draven. He spoke slowly and with great intensity. "If she is truly who this token symbolizes, then you may have just saved our species from eventual extinction."

Draven exchanged a surprised glance with Bailey before asking, "How so?"

"As you know, for many generations, our numbers have dwindled. We lose too many females during the birthing process. Bailey is the one who can save us."

Bailey was shocked. "I don't understand. What do you mean by that, sir? How am I going to save you?"

Kelden moved from behind his large desk and came to sit next to her on the sofa. "Dear child, you are something very special. You will be protected and honored among our people. Your parents knew this; doubtlessly, they died trying to protect you." His words didn't answer her questions, but Bailey was reassured by the calm tone of his voice and the kindness in his eyes. Draven was holding her hand, squeezing it gently.

"I would like to make sure you are in good health and perhaps to take a DNA sample, if I may. Can you and Draven come to the medical lab with me?"

Bailey hesitated for a moment and then rose.

She and Draven followed Kelden through the hallways of the mansion. The walls were red with gold accents; paintings, sculptures, and stuffed animal heads were mounted to the walls at regular intervals.

At the end of the hallway, they came to a room that was larger than it looked; this was the hospital.

Bailey sat on a bed and waited for Kelden to start his examination. She felt like she was going to throw up. It had started while they spoke, a little twinge in her stomach. Suddenly, the wave of nausea was overwhelming. She ran for the trash can, narrowly making it. Kelden exchanged a knowing glance with Draven.

Bailey climbed back up on the bed and lay down, resting her arm over her eyes.

"How long have you been ill, Bailey?" Kelden asked, with a worried look on his face. She did not move as she answered.

"Three days now. I have been dizzy, weak. I just feel off balance. The vomiting is new." Bailey so wanted to just go to sleep. She couldn't remember feeling this bad in her entire life.

"We'll run some quick tests, and then you can go to the guest quarters and get some rest. Any other unusual symptoms?"

Bailey shook her head, already slipping

toward sleep.

After taking her vitals and drawing some blood, Darian and Landon escorted her to a guest room. Kelden and Draven went to the study for a moment and closed the door so they could speak privately.

Bailey was dreaming again.

She was back in the jungle, but this time she was running. The trees towered above her. The ground was a tangle of dried leaves, twigs, and twisted vines. Her feet followed a winding path, running as fast as they could. Everything passed in a blur.

Someone was chasing her. She felt like she was a prey being pursued. She ran faster and faster, her feet hardly touching the ground now. The leaves whipped at her naked flesh as she fled. The dappled sun played tricks in the underbrush, and she lost track of where she was.

Then he was in front of her – the black jaguar, blocking her path. Bailey skidded to a stop to stand before him. Her heart pounded in her ears. She moved toward him, one hand extended. He chuffed, blinked, and licked his lips, and then settled back on his haunches.

She reached out to touch him, and as her hand ran through his plush fur, he became a man. Draven, standing naked before her. He extended a hand and she took it, letting him pull her into him. His arms wrapped around her body. Their lips met in a passionate kiss. His giant cock – it seemed even bigger than normal – pressed against her pelvis. She could feel his desire – it was overwhelming, animalistic, and primal.

His kiss became forceful and needy. He swept her up, and she wrapped her legs around his waist. Her pussy was slick and wet, ready for him. His cock slid into her effortlessly, and he groaned with pleasure. He had both hands on her hands and was bouncing her up and down on his dick. Her breasts jiggled and bounced in his face as her head rolled back.

Draven's grunts became low growls as he thrust harder and faster into her. Her moans became cries and screams.

He threw her down to the soft ground and pounced on her. As her body sank into the moss-covered ground, Draven pounded his dick into her. Her nails raked down his back, raising red welts. She screamed for him to go faster, harder. He answered only in growls and deep, hard kisses.

The orgasm hit her like a tidal wave. It was sudden and overpowering. Ecstasy surged through her body. She couldn't do anything but lay back on the cool, damp ground and surrender.

"Draven, I need to know – do you know anything about her family or her past?" Thinking for a moment, Draven shook his head. Kelden waited a moment before speaking. "Well, it seems that Bailey is much more than she appears to be. She may not understand everything that has happened, but she is the missing link that will help our race survive. I don't know how she found you – perhaps instinct led her to our kind when the time was right. When she was old enough." Kelden paused, letting Draven absorb what he had just said. Then he walked over to the fireplace, lit a candle, and poured two glasses of Scotch, one for himself and one for Draven.

He handed the glass to Draven and sat back down at his seat. "Now I know that you have questions; the answers will show themselves in time. I have questions as well. Did you and she mate by chance? I am not judging. I am just trying to help."

Draven hesitated for a moment. "Yes, why?"

Kelden smiled "That is good. It means that she is listening to her instincts. She is fulfilling her role without even knowing it. I am sure you had your work cut out for you during the transformation, right?"

"Yes," Draven chuckled. "It seemed like her sex drive was truly insatiable."

Kelden laughed. "That's good. It means she is strong."

Puzzled, Draven looked at him. "What do you mean 'strong'?"

Kelden took a drink of his scotch before answering. "Your mate is something very special. She has gypsy blood in her. Mixing her bloodlines with ours will prevent our mates from dying during the birthing process. No one knows why, but when you mix Trigarian blood and gypsy blood, the mothers and their young are tenfold stronger. I would bet that her parents knew that she would find us; that is why they gave her that token. You might know more of this, but the gypsies are very rare people. Centuries ago they were hunted and fled, and no one knew where they went. Her gypsy blood is what causes the strange coloration of her jaguar form.

"She is much stronger than you know. Soon, her senses will be much more sensitive, and she will need to eat much more than you. She will also need much more physical affection, of all kinds, for the next five months or so."

"Why is that?"

"She is expecting, my boy." Kelden laughed as he watched Draven's face turn a ghostly white. He had suspected, but somehow now that it was confirmed, he was overcome with anxiety.

"That's right; you are going to be a daddy. And by my estimation you are looking at five months until she gives birth. I will do an ultrasound before you leave to verify." He paused again, setting down his glass. "She likely would not have been able to give birth to a human child, son. Hybrids like her are often sterile as humans; but mating with one of our kind, going through the transformation, allows them to reproduce."

Still digesting everything, Draven went to the window. "So, if she is what you say she is, what can we do to help her? To keep her safe?"

Kelden walked over to him and put his hand on the young man's shoulder. "We must make sure that nothing happened to her or the young."

"Young, what young?" Bailey walked in, curious as to what they were talking about. As tired as she was, she had been unable to rest long. Her dreams were vivid, and she had woken flushed and agitated. Now, she wanted answers.

"Bailey, love, Kelden needs to talk with you. Come here." Draven sat her down in the chair next to the fireplace. Kelden got down on one knee in front of her so she did not have to look up at him.

"I am just going to come right out and

say it, no sugarcoating. You are a hybrid. You are one of the last of your kind. You were born a gypsy. And now you have become a Trigarian. Your blood is unique. Your genes are what the Trigarians need to survive. The two bloods mixed create a stronger Trigarian. The women and children will survive the birthing process. You are the key to our survival, if you will."

Shock hit her like a ton of bricks. And by the look on his face, she could tell that Kelden was not done with the news yet.

"With that been said, my dear... you are pregnant."

Bailey didn't hear a word he said after that. As he explained the details of a Trigarian pregnancy, all she could think of was, 'How did this happen?' They'd never even talked about having kids. Bailey had always thought she and Draven might have children eventually but only after they were married. 'Does he even want to get married? Man, I really screwed the pooch this time.'

"No, love, you screwed a feline." Draven smiled at Bailey. She blushed. He was reading her thoughts again.

"Don't worry," he said, patting her hand. "We will do what it takes to make it right. If that means getting married the human way, we will do it. But first let's see what the ultrasound says."

She nodded slowly.

The three of them went back into the examination room. Bailey climbed back on the table and lay flat on her back while Kelden pulled the ultrasound machine out and shut off the lights.

"Now relax for a moment and take a few deep breaths." When she was relaxed, he began the ultrasound, moving the paddle over her belly little by little until he found something. As they looked at the screen, there was silence.

Triplets.

Thanking Kelden for his hospitality, Bailey, Draven, and his men started the journey back home. It was going to be an interesting ride; Draven could feel how much Bailey desired him, and now more than ever he did not want to make her wait. He didn't want to feel her wrath when they got home.

The ride home seemed to pass much faster, and before they knew it, they were back in Themeon Forest, setting up camp for the night.

Bailey woke as he laid her on the bed. Her eyes flashed brilliant green, filled with desire. He knew what she wanted; he could hear her thoughts echoing in his head. She licked her lips greedily. He smiled. It seemed her sex drive was ramping up again.

He leaned in to kiss her, and she pulled him down on top of her with a fake growl. As he tumbled down into the bed, he laughed. Things were going to change for them; this, apparently, was not going to be one of those things.

Triplets. He still couldn't get over it.

Her hands were sliding down his body, seeking his half-mast cock. As she kissed down his chest, he was still thinking about the pregnancy. Her lips reached his cock, bringing him back to the moment.

'Pay attention to me, big boy,' she thought, glancing up at him with a smile.

His smile grew wider. She gently caressed his balls. Her tongue traced over the head of his cock, and then she slid his length into her mouth.

Some things would never change.

ABOUT THE AUTHOR

Readers: I want to expand a few of the stories to see where the characters can be explored further. If there are any of the stories that you would like to read more about again, I'd love to hear from you!

Visit my blog at
http://www.trinitystyller.com/

Join my newsletter for free exclusive previews
http://www.trinitystyller.com/in

Follow me on Twitter at
http://www.twitter.com/trinitystyller

Like my page on Facebook at
http://www.facebook.com/trinitystyller

Discover my books at major ebook retailers everywhere.